For the

Silenced

Ones

Charisse Milan

All Scriptures, unless otherwise noted, are from the American Standard Version, published in 1901 by Thomas Nelson & Sons.

All Scriptures marked Amplified are from the Amplified Bible, copyright © 2015 by the Lockman Foundation.

Cover design by Tim Davis

For the Silenced Ones / Charisse Milan

ISBN: 9781734929706

Contents

To the least of these,
those whose voices have been silenced
by abuse.

Acknowledgements

To those who have been brave enough to open bits and pieces of your own stories to me, thank you for trusting me with your hearts. Thank you for offering validation, knowing there is someone else in this world who understands. You truly are my heroes, as we all walk out our freedom together. May all of our voices be returned through the power of Jesus. I love you all.

To my Lord and Savior, the true Jesus Christ, for all the ways He has set me free and taught me what real love is. To my Heavenly Father and the Holy Spirit, for revealing to me more and more of who He is, and who He has created me to be. This journey is forever, forever stepping into more of His love. It's amazing.

To my husband, wow, what a journey we embarked on together. You will never know how much your support has meant to me. You have been my anchor, my best friend, my rock. I am forever grateful for you.

To my children, you are the reason I've put one foot in front of the other and continued my own journey of healing. Thank you for believing in me and loving me through it all.

To my counselor and spiritual "Papa," you showed me what it meant to have a compassionate, loving, safe father, which reshaped my view of God. Thank you for all the time and love you have poured into me, and for teaching me the importance of forgiveness. "Forgive every day, every time, every way, always."

To my editor and new hero, what a fast answer to prayer you were. Your passion for ministering to the least of these, your voice of justice, and your desire to give others back their voice, show me your true love for God and desire to be like Him. I'm forever grateful to you for taking on this project.

To the "Mary" in my life, you've always had my back and have lifted my arms, when I had no strength left. You show me what pressing into friendship, even when it is extremely messy, looks like. Thank you for sticking with me through it all.

To the "Monica" in my life, thank you for stepping into my journey at the right moment, and for the ways your friendship brought a healing balm to my heart. You allowed me freedom to just be.

To my spiritual "mamas," you know who are. Your belief in me, your encouragement over me, and the ways you have demonstrated healthy family relationships have mended me. Thank you.

To my prayer group who have prayed for this book to be birthed, and my other "editor" friends and beta readers who have poured over the pages of my book with me, sometimes pulling the all-nighter, from the bottom of my heart thank you for your input, prayers, coaching, and encouragement.

There have been so many family and friends who have come in my life and been a support and blessing to me throughout the time of writing this book. So many people, more than I can name, that I am forever grateful to, who either walked with me for a short time or the long haul. Thank you for the ways you have touched my life.

Caution for Readers

Though this story is written as adult fiction, it is based on a true story; therefore, many scenes depict things that happen to abuse survivors, especially ritualistic abuse survivors.

I've taken care to avoid as many graphic details as possible for the safety of my readers; however, to tell the story well, certain topics needed to be addressed. For some readers, these topics could cause some symptoms of PTSD.

If you are under the care of a therapist or prayer minister, I urge you to consider getting counsel before reading this book. Though this story is meant for healing, parts of it may cause mental, emotional, or spiritual disturbance.

Because of the nature of ritualistic abuse, the content is highly inappropriate for children and teens.

If you need additional help, you'll find a Resource section at the end of the book, where some hotlines are listed.

I trust that you'll find your own journey to wholeness, and that this book will be a part of that process.

Take a deep breath, and let the journey begin.

Part 1

"When I kept silent, my bones wasted away
through my groaning all day long."
Psalm 32:3

The story you are about to read is based on a true account.

CHAPTER 1

The Dragon

(Spring 1987)

It was a normal Sunday morning, like every Sunday morning Callie could remember in her twenty-seven years of living. Wearing her favorite red dress, she slid to sit in the middle of the wooden pew next to her husband as people crowded in around her.

Instinctively she tucked one arm around her waist while the other hand reached for the cross around her neck. She began to rock back and forth, gazing at the floor.

"Why couldn't we sit farther back?" she whispered to Greg. But he ignored her, turning to shake the hand of the properly-dressed man in front of them.

"Please stand and turn to hymn number 327," said the music director. Mechanically, Callie grabbed the hymnal tucked next to the offering envelopes in the back of the pew. But she clutched her stomach again when she caught a whiff of perfume from the plump lady behind them.

As the piano began to play, her head swam and the room began to spin around like the scrambler at the fair. With trembling hands, she grabbed the pew in front of her, steadying herself.

Am I going to die? Her heart raced as she clumsily sat down and began rocking again, back and forth, to calm herself. She turned her head to the right and then behind. *There's the door. If that's locked, there's a window to that side. I really do know where all the exits are.* She calculated how many people she would have to climb over and how many steps it would take to escape.

As everyone obediently took their places for the sermon, her bouncing legs shook the pew. Annoyed, others shot her looks of disapproval, but she pretended not to notice. *Breathe. Cal, just breathe. You can do this. You do this every Sunday.*

Greg placed his hand calmly on her knee and leaned over to whisper. "Can you please stop shaking your legs? You're embarrassing me." Loosening his tie, he turned his attention back to the man behind the pulpit.

I've got to escape. Have to get out of here. Her chest tightened as the nausea grew. *I can't breathe. Am I having a heart attack?* An image flashed across her mind of herself writhing in pain on the floor, foaming at the mouth while everyone stared at her.

Pull it together, Cal. Come on. She turned her attention again to Greg, but he was engrossed in their pastor's words. "Love your neighbor as yourself."

The urge to run won out. "Greg, I've got to go to the ladies' room. I'll be back in a minute." He patted his approval on her knee.

Trembling and weak, Callie climbed over the people beside her. "Oh, excuse me. So sorry." She mouthed the words to the man whose foot she had just stepped on.

Quickly and quietly, she slipped out the back through the double doors, as they echoed with a dull thud behind her. The fresh air of the foyer hit her hot cheeks, and she breathed a deep sigh of relief.

In the privacy of the bathroom, Callie stared in the mirror to see her usually porcelain skin now an ashen gray. Her bright brown eyes looked back at her, terrified. She sunk her face into her hands.

Why is this so hard? Why do I always feel this way every week? God, where are You?

She stared up at the glaring overhead light. No comfort came. When a well-dressed woman entered the restroom, Callie wiped her smeared mascara and shuffled out to rejoin Greg in the pew, but people were already streaming out of the opened doors.

Thank God.

"Mama. Mama. Look at my picture." Two-year-old Beth lit up the hall as she ran, arms spread open to Callie's embrace. Proudly, she thrust a scribbled picture of animals entering the Ark.

"It's beautiful," Callie said. "Just like you." She pressed her finger gently on Beth's nose.

"Let's go." Greg came around the corner with Star on his hip. "We're going to be late for dinner, and you know how Mom is about her roast." He didn't even ask Callie where she'd been.

That night, Callie fell into a restless sleep.

‹‹∙››

O God, it's back.

Callie hugged her arms tightly across her abdomen. The vein in her neck pulsed hard as she watched the wisps of smoke encircling the rusting cross impaled in the middle of the steeple. Chips of paint dangled from the pointed arms.

Slipping into the church, through the side door closest to the parsonage where her family lived, Callie slunk into the back of the building. The smell of musty air behind the sanctuary made her nose wrinkle with disgust. Her palms sweated as her heart beat out a dull rhythm in her ears.

Callie reached out to run her hands along the smooth cement block walls as a guide, only skipping past the doorways that lined the halls. *Like black holes to dungeon cells.*

On the far left and right, small halls led to the back entrances of the sanctuary. She wouldn't dare go in there, not by herself. She made her way down the hall as quietly as she could, but the sound of her shoes lightly tapping the linoleum tile sharply echoed against the cold, hard walls.

Suddenly fear—like a limp, lifeless hand draped on her shoulder—gripped her, digging its sharp nails into her flesh. The breath of terror filled her lungs.

The dragon.

Seeping from under the doors of the sanctuary, the dragon's sulfur breath poisoned the air around her. She imagined its piercing eyes full of hatred, waiting for her behind the doors.

"Mama, I want Mama," she whispered as she wrung her frail hands. *If I run, it will see me, but at least I can try.*

Callie began to walk briskly, and then broke into a dash. But the dragon's breath flickered on her neck. *I can't make it to the door to get home. Here, I can hide in this classroom.*

There, flannel figures hung out of place on the faded, fuzzy board, the remnants of last Sunday's Noah's Ark story religiously recited from the teacher's manual, lying open on the podium. *No promises here, except of being trapped like a mouse.*

Callie ducked into a corner, breathing heavily. Sweat poured from her brow and stung her eyes. The footsteps of the monster resounded now as they approached the room from down the hall.

"I know you're here," it sneered. As it drew close to the door, Callie could hear the scraping of its long armored tail whipping across the hall.

Found.

Callie dodged the dragon's tail, stumbling, as the monstrosity swung around to face her. Cold needles of fear pricked every nerve.

She fell beneath the hypnotic power of the dragon.

"Callie. Callie, you're dreaming again. Wake up." Greg spoke gently as he prodded Callie.

Abruptly she realized that she was again on her feet with balled-up fists.

"Greg, I'm so sorry." Her heart continued to pound as she sunk back into the bed, fingers wrapped around her aching forehead.

The dream was back.

଼ଓଔଓ

The next morning Callie woke up late, stumbled to get her coffee, and stumbled back to the bedroom to do Saturday chores. Sighing, she looked around her disheveled bedroom.

High in the corners were piled Greg's boxes of old bills, books unread, and receipts long accounted for.

Callie had given up trying to bring order to his chaos, for fear she'd be accused of being like his mother.

Still, chaos on the outside only added to the chaos on the inside. She glanced in the mirror on the other side of the desk. "Speaking of chaos," she muttered. "Ugh." She turned away from the image of herself, with the t-shirt that was somehow tighter than it used to be and the ball cap pulled down over her disheveled brown curls. Unsettled, she glowered at the insurmountable mountain of unfolded clothes waiting for her attention at the end of the bed.

In the corner stood an easel with a blank canvas, unopened paints, and new brushes scattered beneath.

She flung herself face first onto the bed. *Why don't I want to do anything? I'm so very tired.* She rolled over, sat up on the edge, and longingly twirled an empty paintbrush between her fingers. *When will I have the courage to paint what I feel inside?*

Not yet. Not now.

Greg was downstairs, probably watching TV or tinkering with something in the garage like he did every Saturday. He hadn't mentioned the dragon nightmare again. *I guess he packed it up and stored it away like a box in the attic.*

If I'd been a mechanical thing like a car or a computer, he could have fixed me. But I guess since I'm a person, distance seems safer.

❧❀

Another day passed. Another day of struggling to find focus and purpose. Finally it was evening.

"Mama, say prayers?" Callie's daughters called to her from their bedroom.

"I'm coming." Callie opened the door to the nursery where they both lay, Beth in a toddler bed and Star still confined to her crib.

Star pushed up against the side of her crib with arms flown open to her mother's embrace. In response, Callie swept her up into her arms, kissed her on the cheek, and then cradled her on her lap, as Beth crawled up her other leg and sat balancing on her knee.

Callie rocked her two babies, singing softly. "Hush, little baby, don't say a word. . . ." They snuggled in on both sides of her and nodded off to sleep.

She continued swaying back and forth in the chair passed down from her grandmother, listening to the creaking of the wooden joints. While she rocked, she scanned the bookshelf crammed with children's fantasies where she had found escape when she was a little girl: *Winnie the Pooh; The Lion, the Witch, and the Wardrobe; My Father's Dragon;* and *Robin Hood.*

Oh, how my life seems like one of those books. Except it's dusty and forgotten. No one would want to read it with me.

Silently Callie gazed at the worn book covers, wishing she could step into a wardrobe and disappear into another world. *I can't look through my book on my own. I thought Greg might help, but he said the past doesn't affect the present.*

She sighed and tucked her children into their beds.

Quietly she tip-toed to her bedroom, leaving the bedroom door ajar as she had always done. It wasn't safe to close it. With a pen in one hand and journal in the other, Callie withdrew to the old love seat. Normally she relished these moments of solitude with the one she called "Lord," but this night, peace eluded her.

Why am I still struggling with this?

The memory of the dream – the sight of the dragon and the fears it awakened – made her hands tremble. *I'm so afraid, Lord. I feel so alone. Where are You? I know You love me, but I don't feel Your love. I've never been able to feel Your love.*

Tears rolled down her cheeks, the cheeks of a careworn, exhausted young mother. She had just kissed her two children good-night, the two beings she lived for, and yet she barely had the energy to give any of herself to them, much less Greg.

I'm staring down the face of the dragon, and I'm not getting any help from the only one who can help me.

Those two precious children hung in the balance.

It's not time to open the book yet. A quiet voice from within stilled her for the moment.

When, Lord?

Then she cried despondently, "Oh, but I don't think I can let You." Hugging her knees tight to her chest, Callie let out a long trembling sigh. "I can't let you open that book. I'm afraid of what's in it." Her head tilted back toward the ceiling.

She opened her mouth and gave voice to the deepest fear that had been haunting her.

"Dear God, what if I'm the dragon?"

CHAPTER 2

Callie, age 3
Austin, Texas

In the summer of 1962 a sunbaked, winding road led out to a lone country church east side of town, where ripened rows of golden corn waved their heads to the winds. On the horizon, steel giants rose from the flat plains gulping up oil sludge from beneath the crusty earth.

Callie toddled with abandonment through the coarse grass pricking her toes.

"Mama, Mama, can I wash the dog?" Maggie, Callie's only companion, licked at her heels.

"No, Cal. Not now. I've got laundry to hang up. And don't mess with the puppies." Mama shot Callie a sharp look and then proceeded to pin soggy socks, pants, shirts, and towels to limp rope lines yanked from pole to pole.

Nervously, Callie waddled away from Mama's irritation. "Don't mess with the puppies. Don't mess with the puppies." She rehearsed the words, reminding herself of the instructions.

But the simple metal slide felt like it had been set on fire in the mid-day heat of summer. A stream of water from the hose would do a fine job of cooling the steaming metal, and a refreshing pool would provide a splashing end.

So while Mama's back was turned with her mind absorbed into all the things Mamas must think about, Callie grabbed the black plastic bucket, filled it with water, and ran the hose down the slide.

The puppies, those poor little pups. They look so hot. I should help them cool off. With the warning from Mama completely forgotten, Callie gently tucked each puppy under her arm and lifted them to the top of the slide. With padded paws sprawled out, furry balls tumbled down the slide and splashed into the black bucket of mucky water. Delighted and dripping, Callie aided the puppies in their wild ride again and again. Maggie stood beside Callie, yelping.

Finally Mama turned around. To Callie's shock, it wasn't pleasure that filled Mama's eyes—but rage.

Then she heard Mama scream.

Later that evening, Mama sat holding the pups, both of them completely lifeless.

Tears rolled down Callie's hot cheeks—she had only been trying to help them cool off. She reached over to Maggie, solemnly curled at Mama's feet. "I'm so sorry, Maggie," she gasped between sobs. "So very sorry."

ℛℴℛℴℛ

One sultry summer day when Callie was swinging in the back yard, she saw the sky grow dark with swirling clouds swimming in a sea of sickening green.

She had heard Mama refer to the place they lived as Tornado Alley. She had heard grown-ups talking about the spinning, swirling tempest that would leave destruction in its path. Sort of like the swirling on Callie's insides.

Then, as she watched, Callie heard that sound. The sound Mama had warned her about, like a train barreling down the tracks.

From inside the house came Mama's scream. "Run, Callie! Run!"

Callie ran to the storm shelter as fast as her chubby legs could carry her. Mama was already there, flinging open the heavy steel door to the frightening dark pit that looked like a metallic grave.

Which one did she fear more?

Callie hesitated only a moment before Mama pulled her inside, swinging the door shut just behind Maggie, who jumped in with them.

Inside their safe hole they listened to the muffled screeches of the whistling wind outside as Maggie cuddled between them, her doggy breath tickling Callie's nose.

"Thank God," Mama murmured, holding Callie close in her trembling arms.

Then suddenly, all was silent. It was over. As quickly as it had come, it was gone. That was how it always seemed to be.

In the silence Callie's voice sounded too loud. "Where's Father?"

Mama's silence matched the silence of the sky. She never seemed to have an answer. Just a blank look of pain in her eyes.

ಬಿಡುಖ

One source of solace for little Callie was an elderly couple from church, "Tucker and Pops." She loved them. They loved her. And sometimes Mama needed Callie out of the way.

Tucker bustled in the kitchen like a worker bee. "Come, Callie." Steaming rice with sugar and milk sat waiting for her on the counter. It warmed her tummy and her soul. Though her Mama said often that Tucker and Pops spoiled her rotten, Callie relished every moment here, for here she felt like a princess.

Pops bent over to turn the television dial and plopped himself into his rocking chair. "We'll watch your favorite, Callie," he said.

Callie climbed into his cozy lap. The rocking soothed her as Felix the Cat flickered on the small television set in front of them.

Safe. I am safe here.

ಬಿಡುಖ

Fall leaves swirled around barren dirt as the heat of summer subsided. The cool night breezes whistled through the screened windows.

Callie's sweaty brow hung over her bed breathing in the beads of water drifting into the dark air. Her lungs felt hard, somehow. Clutching Mama's hand, she whispered between wheezy breaths, "Mama"—sucking air—"help me."

"Warren." Mama's voice was tight. "We have to get her to the hospital. We have no choice."

Muttering curses, Daddy reluctantly pulled the old station wagon around.

Breathe. Just breathe.

Blurred vision. Darkness.

Mama quietly placed Callie in the back seat and slipped in beside her so she could cradle her head in her lap. All the way to the hospital the two of them sat quiet, just surviving, while the young pastor complained that he had no money for hospital bills.

A blur of frantic emergency personnel, white coats, blinding lights, sirens, all muddled together in Callie's view as she slipped in and out of consciousness. She awoke to find herself in the white, cloudy world of an oxygen tent, with strangers all around. But she was too tired to be afraid.

Then a familiar hand reached in and gently clasped her fingers. It was Tucker! "I have a friend for you to keep you company, Callie."

A funny fellow's red and gray stitched head bopped around the corner of the tent. Callie giggled. "A sock monkey! Mine?" She rocked it close to her heart.

For the months that followed, at times he would be her only companion.

She began to doze off again when she heard her father's voice bellowing through the cold room.

"Pneumonia. This is the seventh time this year!"

CHAPTER 3

The First Meeting

(Summer 1987)

With sweaty palms, Callie sat opposite her pastor's desk, her eyes darting here and there, but mostly looking down at her high-top sneakers.

This man was known for his relational skills, so rather than looming behind the mahogany, he left the plush seat for a simple wooden chair near her. "What's on your mind, Callie?" he asked pleasantly.

Callie's eyes darted toward the door, and as usual, she gauged how many running steps it would take to reach it. Then she saw herself, the great escape artist, doing that very thing and turning to smile at herself from the doorway.

Callie tightly grasped the arms of the seat, but the perspiration from her hands made the leather slippery. "I can't leave my house without panicking," she began. "I've gone to the doctor to get some help, but now I'm pregnant and there's nothing they can give me."

"Callie, you've told me a little of your story already." He cleared his throat. "I know your father was convicted." Apparently he couldn't bring himself to say *pedophilia*.

He cleared his throat again. "I think some professional counseling would be a good thing for you."

Callie's mind looped in a circle. Counseling. She had considered it before. Often she told friends that she had moved fifteen times before she had graduated high school. "Oh, your family was in the military?" some innocent woman would always inquire.

"No. My father was a minister."

Silence usually followed, but one day was different, when one friend had replied, "I'm surprised you haven't needed counseling for that."

The thought of counseling twisted something inside Callie's stomach.

But Pastor Matt continued to explain why he thought this was the right decision for her.

"I have a friend I trust, and I think he can help you. It should take only six to eight weeks to resolve this."

Freedom from these panic attacks in six weeks! Well, that is something to consider. A spark of hope flickered as Callie tried to ignore the glowing red eyes lurking in the shadows of her mind.

"I'll give them a call."

As Callie returned home, her two toddlers tackled her, hugging her legs tightly, begging to be picked up. She lifted Beth to one hip and Star to the other. Star grabbed Callie's necklace, thrusting it into her mouth, but Callie didn't seem to notice. "Mama?" Beth said. But Callie just kissed her little girl and smiled absently. In spite of their constant need for attention, Callie's mind was always somewhere else.

Later that evening, while Greg tried to relax on the sofa with the ball game, Callie paced.

"Callie, you're gonna leave a path in the carpet. Please come and sit by me. Just relax a bit."

She mechanically obeyed, but her legs bounced nervously, upsetting his place of calm.

"Greg, I'm becoming like my mom."

Turning to glance at his despairing wife, Greg said, "Sweetheart, what are you talking about? You're a great mom." He leaned back into the cushion, barricading himself from any discomfort.

"Greg, I love my mom," Callie persisted. "But she's been drugged and numb since I was in college. She can't face anything in life without meds. If I keep going on this way, with these panic attacks, I'll be the same way. We have two babies and another on the way. Greg, I can't do this. I can't become a zombie and raise these kids." She hid her tears with the back of her hand.

Then she added, "Besides, no doctor will drug me with an unborn baby in my womb."

Weird. Why do I feel lightheaded at the word "drug"?

"Oh, I've got to go lay down." She reached for the arm of the sofa to balance herself. "Greg, if I don't get some help I might lose control."

Losing control was not an option.

"What do you suggest, then?" Greg barely glanced away from his ball game.

"Pastor thinks counseling would help."

"Counseling?" Greg turned to face Callie. "Why can't you just push through this?" He squeezed her hand. "I can help you."

"Oh, like on our honeymoon," Callie mused, "when my foot was broken, and you wanted me to just walk it off? Granted, you didn't know it was broken, but that's kind of the point. Greg, I have hardly any memory of my childhood. I don't know what's broken."

"The broken foot story always has to come up, doesn't it?" Greg smirked. "Well, I guess we can give it a try. How long will it take?"

"Pastor says six to eight weeks."

"Just six to eight weeks? That's not so bad. Then you'll be all fixed up."

Later that night, Callie snuggled in bed with a pillow across her lap and her journal open to the next entry. The words spilled onto the page.

Dear Lord, what do You want me to do? I feel over-whelmed. I don't understand why You feel so distant. Why can't I feel You? I don't think I feel much of anything. At least, nothing good. Please help me.

It's time. The thought resounded in her head.

Time for what? Callie's heart beat faster.

It's time to take down the book.

"Oh, God. What does that mean?" Callie gasped. Relief and terror shot through her body, tingling up and down her spine.

What does it mean? What does it mean to take down the book?

Suddenly Callie knew without a doubt she needed to make that appointment for counseling.

ဆဝဢ

Five days later she sat across the table from a Filipino woman that she could barely understand for her "intake interview." From her sex life to the things she had eaten as kid, Callie tried to answer question after question until she felt as if her brain might explode.

Finally the interrogator said, "Well, I think you are fairly normal. We will get you an appointment set up with one of our counselors to see how we can help."

"Fairly normal" sounded good. *Well, that's that.*

Except for the nagging thought that so many questions on the intake had been ones she couldn't answer. Empty blank spaces, like black holes in her memory, especially regarding her father. At best all she had was shadowy impressions.

I wonder if everybody's childhood memories are like that.

The following Tuesday morning when Callie awoke, waves of nausea suddenly washed over her. *Today is my first counseling appointment.*

All morning long she kept gagging.

Should I wear this shirt? No, why in the world would I wear that? This one looks good. No, it looks terrible. Dressy is good. Casual is good. No, no, no.

By the time Callie was dressed, ten shirts and blouses lay in disarray on her bed, and the one she finally chose seemed like a bad decision as soon as she got in the car. Sweat beaded on her forehead, but her hands and feet felt like ice.

Sitting in the van, she waited for the sickening feeling to subside. Then screwing up her courage, Callie prayed, turned the key, and grabbed the steering wheel. The radio began to blare the first lines of "Friend of a Wounded Heart."*

I can do that, Callie thought frantically. *Yeah, I can smile so everybody will think I'm happy. I can lie and say everything is fine. I've been doing that for years.*

She turned up the volume even more, trying to drown out the fears screaming in her mind. She drove gripping the steering wheel so tightly that her fingers began to ache.

As she pulled into the parking lot she thought grimly, *The hospital is less than a mile away from this place. I could get there in less than five minutes.* Somehow making an escape plan always helped her feel better.

Gaining composure, Callie straightened her shirt and reluctantly approached the door. As she sat with her heart pounding, her eyes focused on the exit sign. *Why is this so hard?*

"Welcome." Dr. Galloway appeared, a medium-sized older woman with gray hair pulled back from her face. She smiled.

Callie meekly followed her into a simply decorated office where a picture of Jesus washing Peter's feet hung on the wall.

As Callie tried to answer Dr. Galloway's questions about her father, an odd feeling crept over her body, frightening her. As the discomfort grew, she shifted back and forth in her chair.

"What are you feeling, Callie?" Dr. Galloway straightened her steel-rimmed glasses.

"I don't know," Callie muttered. "Weird. Like something is touching me. Down there."

---

*Claire Coninger and Wayne Watson, "Friend of A Wounded Heart." © Warner Chappell Music, Inc., 1987.

"That's a body memory," Dr. Galloway explained. "Were you abused?"

"I wasn't abused," Callie shot back. "I was kept safe in a bubble. I don't remember ever being abused." She fought back the returning waves of nausea.

As the session continued, Callie continued to withdraw, answering more and more questions with "I don't know."

The book will stay sealed.

The doctor gently leaned in, and Callie glanced up to see her kind face. "Callie, there's a reason you have a lot of blank spots. Your mind is trying to protect you. It's what it does when a little girl thinks she can't handle what's happening to her. You're safe now, and it's OK."

Protective mechanism. Protective parts of my mind. It all makes sense somehow.

But now someone knew how her mind worked.

Escape! Her mind screamed.

There was the door. The master escape artist could do it. If the door was locked, she could move to plan B or plan C.

Her breath came in short gasps. *What was plan B?*

Instead of running, Callie turned to stone in the chair.

"Breathe, Callie. Just breathe," came the gentle instructions.

"Callie, our time is up," Dr. Galloway said, as she finished writing her notes. "I'll see you next week." She smiled and stood up, straightening the jacket of her business suit.

Callie stood up too, trying to straighten her shirt. She looked at the floor, daring to glance up at the smiling doctor, mumbled a thank-you, and left.

Three months passed. Three months of weekly counseling appointments that grew perhaps slightly less terrifying and slightly more bearable. Three months of hearing "Friend of a

Wounded Heart" play every time she drove to her appointment.

Not much changed over that time. Not much except that, like a sleeping giant disturbed, something inside began to slowly awake.

CHAPTER 4

Bubbles

(Fall 1987)

"Dr. Galloway, this is a picture of my two girls." Callie fumbled through her wallet, pulling a worn photo from the inside pocket. "The two-year old is Beth, and the one-year old is Star."

"They're beautiful girls. Almost like twins."

Callie admired the neat trim of Dr. Galloway's polished fingernails as she handed her the photos. Instinctively she curled her own fingers into fists, hiding the jagged edges of her nail-bitten fingertips. She squirmed in the chair across from this counselor, whom she was beginning to call friend.

"Callie, I don't normally do this, but I'd like you to have my personal phone number if you need anything. You can call me anytime you need to. I think you need to have that assurance."

"Thank you, Dr. Galloway. I won't abuse that privilege."

"I know you won't. I trust you."

Trust me. Why would anyone do that? I don't trust myself.

A breeze of hopefulness swept over her as she pulled out of the driveway.

Only a few days later, Greg took a call from the counseling office. Reluctantly, he turned to his worried wife. "Honey, they need to get you set up with another counselor. Dr. Galloway quit yesterday."

"What? That can't be." Stunned, Callie slumped down at the kitchen table. "But she just gave me her number. I thought I could trust her."

Her thoughts began to muddle chaotically, and a loud ringing in her ears drowned out her children's voices in the next room.

Too much. I was too much for her.

"I don't think I can do this again, Greg. I can't start over with a new counselor."

But she knew she had already passed a point of no return. She had cracked opened the book.

ಬಾಣ

"It should be an easy fix," they had said. "Six to eight weeks," they had said.

Now she was sitting in a new office with a man she'd never met before last month.

Callie had been willing to open the book, but then she just wanted to plow through it as quickly as possible. *Why is each chapter so tightly sealed? Why is it so hard to find out what's in it? Why is six weeks turning into six months with no end in sight?*

"Callie. Callie."

Callie slowly lifted her head to look at Mike, her new counselor.

"How did you view your childhood?"

She stared at him blankly.

"Callie, try to focus. How did you view your childhood?"

This was her third session with Mike, and all of them had been extremely difficult. She always tried to see where the exits were, always tried to have an escape plan. But when she sat in front of him, her mind grew fuzzy, her vision blurred, ringing deafened her ears, throbbing drummed in her head, and visions of sudden disaster tumultuously crashed across the screen of her mind.

Why am I doing this to myself? Will this never stop?

Suddenly, a sinister voice added to her own. *You're killing yourself. Why don't you just give up?*

Callie struggled to answer, as if she were coming up from underwater, as if she had cotton stuffed in her mouth.

"Like a bubble," she mumbled. "I was in a bubble. I knew bad things were happening around me, but I couldn't exactly see what they were. The bubble prevented me."

Her thoughts cleared a little, and her speech became more natural. "Things didn't hurt me, because I was safe inside. I've tried to work through what I know, but most of it I don't remember. There are just blank spaces. Lots of blank spaces."

Trembling, she raised her copper eyes to meet Mike's. "Is that good enough?"

It has always worked well. Why mess with a good system? Besides, what might become of me if I should see what was beyond the milky film?

But bubbles always pop one day, always leaving a splattery mess.

"Callie, why do you think the bubble was there?"

"I suppose to protect myself." Callie felt her head filling with chaotic confusion again.

"Listen. I'm here to help you. Not hurt you. And yes, you evidently were trying to protect yourself."

Mike paused, but then slowly continued. "Callie, what we want is not just to pop the bubble, but we want to ask God to come into whatever painful place there is that you were trying so hard to protect yourself from. When He comes into that place and you choose to forgive, then He'll replace the lies you believed with truth and heal your wounded heart."

Mike leaned across his desk and folded his hands. It was Callie's turn.

I don't know if I can even trust God to show up, and if He does, what then? I can't let Him see. The eternal one watching my bursting mess? No.

She shook her head and walked out of the office.

છગ

Callie arrived at her next appointment with her ball cap pulled low over her unbrushed hair to hide her bloodshot eyes. As she leaned back in the seat with her head stiff, her legs shook violently.

Mike appeared not to notice. "OK. I'd like to ask you to repeat this after me so we can see where the root of this anxiety is coming from." He leaned forward. "Jesus, take me back to the first time I felt afraid like this."

"Jesus." She fought against the rising panic. "Take me back to the first time I felt afraid like this."

A page began to turn.

The heaviness in her chest weighed like a stack of bricks.

Am I having a heart attack? Is this going to kill me?

Her eyes twitched, but an image slowly began to emerge in her mind, like swimming through murky water.

You'll die if you see this. You'll lose your mind.

Slowly, steadily—and unexpectedly—an outline appeared of a young man holding a two-year-old. *It's me. That little child is me.* She saw him grasping her, perpetrating on her.

The shadowy details blurred, but she still felt his hot breath on her delicate neck. Her skin began to crawl, and she flinched.

"I hate him! I hate him! Let me go!" She batted the air wildly with flailing arms.

Even as the tiny girl tried to wriggle free, the abuser in her memory clasped her in a firm grip, his voice smooth and sickening. "You're my little sweet thing now. Your daddy gave you to me."

She felt him lick her neck. Callie jerked violently and pulled herself into a ball. The scene went dark.

From out of somewhere, a gentle voice spoke. "Callie, are you willing to invite Jesus into this memory with you?"

Callie could barely manage a nod.

Immediately, she saw another figure come up and take her from those perverse hands. He held little Callie gently, but when she tried to look in the face of her rescuer, all she could envision was more of the same.

She just wanted to be set free.

The book slammed shut.

"Callie, that's all for today." Mike's voice pulled her back into the present. "But I want you to know something."

He slowed his speech. "You may be what we call one of the least of these."

"Wait, it's been almost two hours?" Callie shook herself in disbelief. "It seemed like just a few minutes." She paused. "What does that mean? The least of these?"

"In the Bible, Jesus said, 'whatever you've done to the least of these, you've done it unto Me.' Well, there are certain clients we call 'the least of these.' By the way you're reacting, I think you might be one of these, but I'll explain that later. We'll try to get further next time."

As Callie drove home, she worried. *What did he mean by that?* Then another thought flashed through her mind. *Would God really treat me like the man in the image? If God would abuse me, then what's left?*

Anxiety surged over her like a tidal wave.

There would be nothing worse than that, nothing left to hope for, nothing that could save me.

All her adult life she had been running from the dragon, like he still had some magical hold on her. She'd hidden so she wouldn't have to see a horror movie. She had covered her face, averting her eyes in movie rental stores, so as not to view the gruesome images on the covers. Anything having to do with darkness terrified her.

But what if the enemy is God after all? As if she'd swallowed a boulder, Callie's stomach ached with the heaviness of the thoughts.

৪০৫৪

"Mommy, read this?" Beth tugged on her shirt. It was *Green Eggs and Ham,*[*] an easy one to read aloud while her mind ran in all different directions, because the girls knew it

---

[*] Dr. Seuss, *Green Eggs and Ham.* Random House, 1960.

by heart. Callie nodded, and they both came to snuggle next to her.

"I am Sam," Callie began.

"Sam I am," Beth continued.

She pictured an ant hill that had been kicked, with thousands of ants scrambling in every direction. *That's my mind.*

"Do you like green eggs and ham?" they chorused together.

Callie continued reading without seeing the words.

I can't even focus on changing a diaper. I barely remember to feed them. My brain is chaos. What's going on? Why is this happening? I used to be able to hold everything in neat boxes in my mind. What happened to all of them?

Wham. The ant hill image flashed before her again. Thousands of tiny pieces.

"Mommy? Turn the page."

"Ummm . . . Would you like them in a house?" Callie read.

"Would you like them with a mouse?" Beth said.

Somehow they made it through the rest of the book.

ഇൗരു

After dinner, Callie stood washing the dishes with her back to Greg, who sat at the table, staring at her.

Finally he spoke. "Why do you have to keep doing this? If you forgot all that stuff, it was for a good reason. And you don't need to try to dig up the past. It's the past. You just need to keep your eyes on the road ahead. If you keep looking behind, you'll wreck."

"That's all fine and good, Greg, except now I can't think straight." Callie didn't turn to face him, but her back stiffened. "I feel I'm losing my mind most of the time. What do I do?

I've opened up this, this book. How can I just shut it again? I just want to be at peace, to feel normal, whatever that is, but I can't go back now."

Greg was silent. Like strings on a violin growing more taut with each turn of the pegs, the tension grew.

All I really want is a normal life, whatever that is. Wiping dirty bottoms, trips to the zoo pushing a double stroller, sleepless nights comforting sick children, the cry of "Mama, I need you," and dinner to fix. *Is that a normal life?* She grimaced. *My friends might think that's what I'm living now, but it seems unreachable.*

Then new thoughts began to intrude.

Greg has never understood you. He's just being selfish. It's all about the money. He doesn't want you to get help. She found herself agreeing with the thoughts.

Star let out a yelp from the living room, as Beth pushed her to the ground. As usual, Greg jumped up. "Now, girls, behave yourselves," he said kindly. "Mommy is tired. Off to bed, both of you." Whisking them up in his arms, he carried them down the hall.

I wish he could do that for me, swoop me into his arms and soothe all my troubles away. I wish he could care for me as easily as he does them.

She cradled her tummy, wondering what the effects of all the trauma of digging up bones was having on her little one who was yet unborn. Was that why she'd been diagnosed with gestational diabetes? *Dear God, am I harming our little one?*

Guilt tinged her heart as condemning words rang in her ears. *Yes. You fool. You should never have opened this up now. Damaged, she will be. Your fault.*

Her eyes lifted to heaven, but no answer came.

Gently rubbing her belly, Callie tried to speak comfort to the baby inside. "Dear one, what I'm going through is all my own stuff. It doesn't have to do with you. Please little one, don't be afraid."

ဆာသ

That night was the same as so many nights had been lately. When she should have been peacefully sleeping, Callie watched "things," black shadowy things, fall on her and nearly suffocate her. Or she would see a dark figure standing at her door.

That night a shadowy serpent slithered up next to her. Instinctively, she grabbed a dagger from somewhere and jammed it into its head. It vanished like green vapor.

She trembled as the vision ended. *I have to protect my children from these demons, but how?*

As she closed her eyes and leaned her head back into her pillow, an image of white feathers gently wrapped around her. *Callie, this angel will not leave you during this time. You are covered under My wings.*

Will You protect my babies? I have to protect them.

But, Lord, I feel like I have to protect them from me.

What if the demon is in me?

She glanced over at Greg, snoring loudly next to her.

He has no idea.

ဆာသ

"Why do you feel you need to continue with this counseling or prayer ministry or whatever you call it? Are you getting healing? Do you feel relief?"

It had been months since Callie had talked with, Edith, her seasoned Sunday school teacher who also happened to be a manager at Bloomingdale's.

She had thought it would be a good idea to have lunch with her, to regain some sense of balance.

But now she wasn't so sure.

Edith's eyes bored into Callie the way they did, as she waited for an answer.

Callie felt herself stumbling over her words. "In some ways, yes," she stammered. "But before I leave the office, something else starts to rise up. Mike says there will be an end to it. But I have no idea when."

"Jesus sets us free. He doesn't lead us into bondage. This seems like bondage, Callie."

As the pressure of scrutiny mounted, a cloud of confusion swirled in Callie's mind.

"I know He does. I believe that. But I feel like a caterpillar that's gone into its cocoon. All the parts have been disassembled and are a big jumbled mess."

"But that means that God will reassemble the mess into a beautiful butterfly. There is hope in that."

Callie looked at her, puzzled.

But Edith was gathering her purse and briefcase to go on to her next appointment. The conversation had come to a decisive close.

Callie left the diner more confused than when she had arrived. *Maybe that wasn't quite the thing I needed to help me regain my sense of balance.*

ॐ

Two months later, Callie finally held her new baby in her arms. With the sweet scent of little Alaia's silky brown hair, Callie nuzzled her forehead to her face, kissing it.

"She looks just like my grandfather," she said with amazement. "Definitely Honeywell blood in her. Just look at her scrunched up face, so square, and two dimples." Looking into Greg's clear blue eyes, she continued. "She was kissed by angels. That's what my mom always said."

Suddenly tears welled up in her eyes. *So beautiful, so perfect. So much unlike me. All I am is broken. A broken mess.*

The "broken mess" seemed to be confirmed once more as the days after Alaia's birth brought sleeplessness, with Alaia screaming for the satisfaction Callie's breast somehow couldn't provide.

"Callie, just put her on the bottle. You're too exhausted to keep doing this." The voice of her sister's reason on the phone finally won her over.

Eva is right. I have nothing to feel guilty about. . . . So why do I keep feeling so guilty? "Greg, please let me call Mike. He can help me."

Greg's lips tightened. "And I'm not enough."

"Please, honey. He'll know how to help these . . . these crazy feelings." With her tired, red-streaked eyes begging, Greg conceded stiffly. "All right. Call him if you have to."

In a moment she had dialed the memorized number. "Mike?" she weakly said into the phone. "I can't sleep at all."

"Is it just the baby keeping you up?"

"I feel anxious. I can't take care of my kids. It feels like things are out of control."

"Do you feel like you have to keep control, Callie?"

"Yes. If I don't, I don't know what will happen." She began to sob.

"This will just be a band aid, but I want to ask you something. Who inside feels like you have to keep control?"

Unexpectedly, an answer came from somewhere deep within her. "I have to."

"Why?"

"If I don't, Callie will lose her mind. I have to stay in control."

"It sounds like there may be someone inside that feels like they have to stay in control and won't let Callie sleep."

Callie had never heard anything like this before. *What's he talking about?*

But Mike continued. "For example, a child who feels out of control can create a part of her that does the job of keeping things in control. The problem is as you grow older, these parts continue to do the job you assigned them as a child to do, and as an adult you don't even realize it. But Jesus heals the brokenhearted, and He puts all these pieces back together again. So what we'll do now is ask Him to heal this part of your mind."

"That makes sense." Callie's voice shook. "But I feel afraid."

"It's all right, Callie. When you get your strength back, we'll find why you felt you needed to take control, but for now, let's ask Jesus to bring this part of you to peace. Just repeat after me, 'True Lord Jesus, would you come and speak to this part of me that has to take control? What do You want this part to do?'"

Callie repeated the words. Then she heard a calm, soothing voice. "I want you to be at peace, little one."

"Callie," Mike asked. "Will this part of you let Jesus take the job of being in control, and give her the job of being at peace?"

"Yes. Please, Jesus bring peace to me."

Immediately, shalom washed over her mind and spirit. Callie thanked Mike, hung up the phone, and soon fell into a deep sleep. A temporary peace.

CHAPTER 5

Callie, age 4

Austin, Texas

"Come on. Follow me," Callie called to her little friend. The blonde-haired, blue-eyed girl obediently followed the pastor's daughter down the narrow hallway of the church to the fellowship hall. Sneaking into the kitchen, Callie found the treat she was seeking: leftover grape juice and crackers from the morning's communion ceremony. With childish pleasure, the two girls snacked.

But Callie's father's condemning words echoed in her ears. *If you take this unworthily, you will bring a curse on yourself. You will get sick and die.*

The thought made Callie's stomach twist, and the juice and crackers didn't hold the same pleasure they had just a few minutes before. She wiped her mouth with the back of her hand and motioned for her friend to leave that place with that evil temptation.

ಐಂಜ

She was the pastor's daughter. And as the pastor's daughter, you had certain things expected of you. It was just understood.

"Don't slouch. Stop twirling your dress in your fingers." Mama was teaching her four-year-old daughter the 23rd Psalm. Day after day Callie had recited the comforting words. Mama didn't say much, but Callie could tell from her grim smile that she was pleased.

"Now get outside. Get out from underfoot."

Callie didn't need to be told twice. She flew out of there like a bird let out of its cage. "C'mon, Maggie!"

Together they ran to the field between her home and their church, laughing at the brisk wind. Suddenly Callie stopped and grabbed Maggie's collar.

"There's Father."

The little girl got a sick feeling in her stomach. He was almost never home, it seemed like, and she hadn't known he was there.

But he didn't see her. He was setting fire to the trash in the large metal drum.

The wind whipped through the tall grasses as a tongue of flames licked the sky. Without warning, the lick of the tongue sparked up and out, igniting the dry ground. Within seconds the grass began to blaze, and Callie saw the fiery hell she was always hearing father yell about from the pulpit.

"Mama! Mama!" she screamed, running into the house. "Father is burning down the church!"

Mama grabbed the phone to call the fire department. Callie watched the fire lurch dangerously to the church doors, but soon men showed up with hoses and buckets of water, frantically yelling and running from church to house and back again. Smoke burned Callie's eyes as they too seemed to catch on fire. Her lungs, already weak from the inflammation of asthma, tensed; her chest felt tight like leather stretched over a drum.

Finally the sweaty, scorched men left one by one. Thankfulness and relief filled the air. Nothing lost.

Later that evening, Callie cuddled next to Mama. "Mama, where's Father?"

Mama's body stiffened. "I don't know, Cal. He said he needed to go visit a friend in the city. He'll be home Sunday morning in time to preach. Just rest."

Callie tried to snuggle, but with the new baby growing in her mama's tummy, no position was comfortable. She looked up into Mama's weary, swollen eyes.

Callie's heart broke. It always seemed when they needed Father, he was never there. Just her and Mama. They were all alone.

She was all alone.

℘〜℘

But maybe it was better for Father to leave them alone. Whenever he was home, something about his presence made Callie squirm and want to hide.

The little girl didn't have words to describe how he made her feel, but "safe" was not a feeling she knew in his presence.

"Come here, Callie," Father demanded. "Come sit on my lap." Then he added, "I'll have a surprise for you later."

A catch of excitement welled in her chest. *He has a surprise for me? He cares about me!*

But somehow something else was there too. Dread?

Excitement and dread? Callie felt filled with confusion.

Father pulled Callie up on his lap, hugged her close, and started touching her in that way he did, a way that always felt strange. "I love you," he whispered in her ear. But the words seemed to hold a twisted meaning.

Is this what love is supposed to feel like?

But it was the only "love" from her father Callie had ever known. So once again she disappeared inside, the way she was used to doing. She couldn't hide her body, but she could hide her soul.

‍‍

Callie stood with her parents at the registration counter at the hospital.

"It's time for your baby brother or sister to come," Mama explained.

"Please, Mama, don't leave me." Callie tried to hang on to Mama's skirt. "I'm scared."

"No, you go with Father. You'll be fine." Mama pushed her away and sat down in the wheelchair a nurse offered. She waved to Callie as the nurse wheeled her down the hall.

She doesn't want me. I don't have any choices.

Callie was left with her father and found out what "surprises" he had been promising her before. As she cried out in pain, his hot breath filled her ear. "This is our secret. You won't tell anybody. If you tell, then your mama and the new baby will die."

They can't die. If I tell and they die, it will be my fault. Callie did her very best to disappear again. That way she could forget the pain. She could forget the horror. She could forget all of it.

A couple of days later, her father woke her early. "Callie, get up. Tucker's here to get you."

Callie couldn't even express the relief in her heart that she felt to see the kind elderly woman from church.

Father left, and Tucker swung the little girl to her hip.

Callie winced.

"Baby, what's wrong? Does something hurt?" Tucker's concerned expression looked like Callie should remember something.

But she didn't.

"I'm fine, Tucker," she said, forcing a smile.

ಬಂಧ

In the following weeks, whirlwinds of activity filled the little house. Items lay helter-skelter everywhere, filling boxes and overflowing them.

Every moment possible Callie spent gazing at little Eva and gently touching her. *What a sweet little baby!* If she had remembered the secrets, she wouldn't have told them for Eva's sake. But she didn't remember them. They were gone.

"Mama, read a book?" she asked.

"I don't have time. We're moving, Callie," Mama said. "We're going to live in a new house."

"But why are we moving, Mama?"

"We just are."

When the doorbell rang, Callie peeked out the window to see an old woman. Mama's face lit up as she ran to the door to open it.

The old woman reached out her arms to the little girl, who backed away. "I'm Me-Ma, Callie." She slowly crouched down to talk to the little girl. "Do you remember me from all the treasures I've sent you through the mail?"

Callie nodded slowly, and her eyes began to light up. *So this is the woman behind all those presents.*

"I've brought another one." Out came a large box with a big festive bow.

All her fears gone, Callie pulled at the bow and paper to open the box. She squealed with delight to find a beautiful handmade red dress.

"Thank you, Me-Ma!" Callie hugged her tight, and Me-Ma hugged back. *This is what love feels like. I never want to let go.*

Me-Ma helped her little granddaughter change into the red dress, and Callie twirled and twirled. But suddenly Mama called sharply, "Callie, quit that playing and get over here and help me with this packing."

"Sweetheart." Me-Ma gently patted Mama on the arm. "Let Callie be a little girl. You treat her like an adult. She's only four."

"But I need her help, Mom, and you always said spare the rod, spoil the child. You can see I need help."

"But where's Warren? He should be here to help you pack."

"I don't know. He's gone again." Mama looked down at all the boxes, her thin lips set in a straight line.

With lips pursed, Me-Ma took off her coat and began quietly helping Mama fill boxes.

A few days later, Mama, Eva, Callie, and Me-Ma all boarded a plane for their new home in Florida, and still Father was nowhere in sight. As the plane rose into the air, Callie pointed to the fluffy clouds. "Is this where the angels live, Mama?"

"Yes, Callie. They live in the clouds."

Callie hugged her sock monkey close to her heart, pressing her nose up against the cold glass window. "Will I ever see Tucker and Pops again?"

"I don't know, honey." Mama sighed, pulling Callie closer to her side while rocking Eva in her arms.

I miss them so much. Tears wet the top of the gray, plush head beneath her chin. Callie stared out the window and tried to imagine dancing with angels on the clouds.

CHAPTER 6

Bursting

(Spring 1988)

A spring breeze blew through the cherry tree that was bursting into bloom at the lake where Callie sat at a picnic table holding a giggling Alaia. Beside her sat her mom, smiling at Beth and Star as they chased the annoyed geese.

"Such energy. I wish I had half of it." It seemed like these days every time they got together Mom's weary face showed more sad wrinkles from her life of worry and trauma.

Callie chuckled, trying to lighten the mood. "Those colors they're wearing make them look like fat butterflies."

"If anybody found a way to bottle up energy like that, they'd become a millionaire." Mom sighed, apparently having no time for flighty metaphors.

Callie breathed deeply and looked up. *OK, this time I really am going to ask her the question I've been needing to ask.*

"It's a perfect day," she began. "Those clouds remind me of the clouds out the airplane window when we flew from

Austin to St. Pete when I was four. You told me the clouds were where angels lived. Remember that?"

"I don't remember that. Doesn't seem like something I would say."

Ugh. Talking with Mom always hurts my heart. Callie cleared her throat and tried again. "How are things at your apartment complex?"

"Same as always."

Cooing to Alaia or calling to the other girls eased the tension. But finally Callie decided it was time. *Mom has so many secrets, and I've got to get to some of them. But I have to sound nonchalant. If I sound too curious, she won't answer me.*

"Mom, there's something I've been thinking about. I was just wondering if you remember anyone I might have been around when I was little that concerned you." *Good, I kept my tone neutral.*

"Well." Her mom hesitated before replying. "There was a group of people your dad invited to the church one summer. I always felt really uncomfortable around them, like there was something wicked about them."

"Oh? Can you tell me more about them?"

Too curious. I sounded too curious.

"No, there's no use in that. The past is the past. We don't need to talk about it." Mom folded her arms the way she did and started swinging her leg.

The girls chased the geese into the water, pelting them with bread crumbs. Delighted, Alaia clapped her chubby hands.

I'm so sick of secrets. But at least that's a clue.

ഇരുഃ

"Greg, I hurt all over." Callie snapped the lids of leftover containers and shoved things around in the refrigerator to fit them inside. "Every cell in my body aches."

Greg slipped up behind her, gently caressing her. As the months had passed, he seemed to better understand what Callie was dealing with, and he was no longer telling her to "just tough it out."

Relaxing, Callie let herself go limp in his arms, laying her head against his shoulder. Her sobs muffled in his shirt while he held her.

"I don't know what to do. I feel like I'm being pulled apart on the inside. I can't do this. It's killing me. I just want to be free."

"Babe, I'd fix it all if I could. You know that, right?"

She released her tension into his touch, feeling his compassion flowing into her.

"Sweetheart, all I know is we keep going forward. You know this is the path God led you to. We just have to trust Him."

Easy for him to say.

But she knew he was right. There was no turning back now.

"Maybe putting on music in the evenings would help. It seems like the evenings are hardest for you. Whatever happens, Callie, I'm right here, and I'm not leaving. Everything will be all right. I promise."

Callie wiped her eyes and blew her nose, ignoring the emptiness of Greg's promise. "All right, Greg. I'll try some music."

Greg put a cassette tape in the player, and Callie's feet found the rhythm on the kitchen floor as the melody lifted her heart. She twirled her girls around and round, singing about our awesome God. Beth and Star laughed as they spun around, their feet slipping beneath them on the slick floor. Alaia clapped her hands on the high chair tray.

Smiling at the scene, Greg hummed in the doorway. The oppression began to lift a little, for now.

☙❧

A few days later, here she sat at the small diner across from Edith again.

In her designer suit, heels, and perfect make-up, Edith sat stiffly at the table with her legs crossed, facing Callie.

Callie . . . in her t-shirt, faded jeans, and favorite ball cap pulled down over her swollen eyes.

"You need someone besides me to talk to about what's going on," Greg had said one night when she'd been sobbing uncontrollably. "You know, processing."

Callie glanced up at Edith and then back down, stirring her coffee way more than it needed.

"What's going on, Callie." It was more of a statement than a question.

"All I see . . . is a large black hole in front of me . . . and me falling into it."

Callie ventured a glance up at her friend.

"Callie, what do you mean?" Edith's voice was testy as she impatiently brushed out of her way a graying wisp of almost-perfectly coiffed hair.

Tears welled up. "I don't know if I'm going to make it."

Edith almost slapped the table. "Callie, you are not going to die." Her voice was low but intense. "You have to think of your three girls and Greg. You have to fight for them."

*But I **have** been thinking of them, and how much better off they'd be without me.* Callie tried to hide the tear that slipped out. *I don't want to hurt them. I don't want to leave them.*

"Your family needs you. Snap out of this."

I wish it was that easy to snap out of it. Callie looked up with desperate eyes. *No one understands.*

Note to self: Meeting with Edith. Bad idea.

As she drove home, Callie remembered Mike's urging. "Let Jesus in with you. He'll bring you life."

But letting Him in means I have to open all of the book. And that feels like death, not life. What if I don't make it? What if looking at what happened to me kills me? Or worse, what if it destroys my family? The voices continued to scream the questions in her head.

Yet, every time she prayed, she heard the gentle voice. "Callie, I won't hurt you. Let Me read the book with you."

But trusting anyone, even God, went against everything she felt.

ᎴᏨᏣ

"What are you so afraid of, Callie?" Mike was asking. Probably because she had rolled her chair across the room near the door, as far as possible away from Mike.

I dunno. Maybe it's that I had to walk all the way to the back of the building because of that dumb dance recital in the auditorium. Maybe it's because there's no security camera in here. Maybe because I feel like I'm going to die.

"I don't know. I feel like I'm going to die." Both of her legs were shaking violently.

"Callie, let's talk for a minute." His calm voice soothed her, like talking her away from the edge of a cliff. "I know this is hard for you, but what keeps you bound up is the lies you've believed about what happened to you."

"But I've forgiven. Why do I have to see what happened?"

"Callie, sometimes a wound is so deep and festering that it needs to be opened to be cleaned out. You have an extremely painful and deep wound. If you don't let God heal it, it may just go septic on you."

"I'm not a bitter person," Callie shot back.

"That's not what I'm talking about. What this person did was sin and a crime, and justice is appropriate. But forgiveness is your releasing that person to God, to let Him be the judge, because as long as you personally hold onto him, it's as if you're tied to him. All I'm asking you to do is step out of the way and let Jesus take it from here."

He took a deep breath and continued, "Callie, I know you don't want to have to see what happened, but you're already in pain. If you're willing to see it all, then in the long run, your pain will lessen."

His words finally broke through.

Yes, she was still living in the pain, and the pain was slowly killing her.

"I don't know if I can."

"Yes, you can. He was already with you, Callie, and you have already lived through this once. You survived it then, and you can survive it now."

But the words she had been told as a little girl screamed in her mind. *You will die, and I will destroy your family if you ever tell.*

A well-guarded fortress stood between her and release. Ultimately she had to make the choice to stay in bondage or to begin the long walk out.

Callie took a deep breath. "I'm ready. Let's try." She closed her eyes and asked the question. "Jesus, take me to the source of this pain. Take me to the root."

For a time, she saw nothing. Then she asked the next question. "Why do I not want to see this? What will happen if I do?"

You will die! Again came the fierce words from somewhere deep within her.

"Jesus, will I die?" she countered.

No, child. I will be with you. Take My hand and let Me into your book.

Back and forth, back and forth they went. It was so hard to be able to trust, but finally the guard inside her relented. *OK. I'll let you see.*

Callie sweated profusely as her heart beat wildly in her chest. What would she see?

Vaguely, a long hallway came into focus. Bright, hazy light. There was her father standing at the end by the fellowship hall door, beckoning her to come.

"I have a surprise for you, Callie." His smile was twisted.

She missed the smirk as her heart beat with anticipation of a good surprise.

"A party?" She reached for the doorknob.

And her father pushed her into hell.

Dizzy. Spinning. Sinking. She stood frozen alone in the center of the outline of a pentagram, surrounded by hooded creatures. Icy cold fingers gripped her throat.

She tried to focus on her surroundings, but everything remained clouded. Trembling with terror, she saw what looked to be white shrouded beings with dark holes for eyes, encircling her.

Chants. Moans. Indistinguishable words.

"Callie, what's happening? Talk to me." Mike's voice came from some faraway place.

"Umm." She licked her dry lips. "It's like I'm in the middle of some kind of satanic thing." Words sounded hollow.

Mike's voice was still firm. "Ask Jesus to join you there."

As Callie's lips tried to form the words, her heart raced. Sweat dripped off her forehead. Tears streamed down her cheeks.

Suddenly, she saw figures of light behind each hooded being. They seemed to be holding them back from her.

Angels? She couldn't remember seeing them before, but she began to calm for just a moment. Then she looked to her right at the table.

Her father came to her. *Will he save me?*

But instead, he grabbed her up, coldly whispered something in her ear, forced her down on the table, and stripped her of the precious red dress her grandma had made for her. After roughly tying her hands, he pushed her face down on the table.

Suffocating heaviness. Hot breath. Sweat. *I'm going to explode.* She heard screams from across the room.

In the office, Callie slammed her chair into the wall trying to get away from a predator only she could see. "God, please just let me die. Please just let me die."

Mike's strained voice pierced through the darkness. "Callie, can you ask Jesus where He is?"

"Jesus, help me," was all she could say.

Immediately she saw Jesus lying face down in front of her. Nose to nose, His beautiful face almost touched hers. With tear-filled eyes, He asked, "Callie, can I take your place?"

"I can't. I can't do that to You."

"You aren't doing this to Me. They are. For what they have done to the least of these, they have done to Me."

In a moment, Callie saw herself sitting on the edge of the table. And there was Jesus, lying with His scarred hands tied, taking the suffering that had been given to her. Disbelief and shame overwhelmed her.

The next moment, she saw the Son of God sitting beside her, swinging His legs over the side of the table in rhythm with hers. He gazed into her eyes, His own like crystal light, penetrating every cell of her being.

"I'm so sorry they did this to you, sweetheart."

"But I must have deserved to be treated this way."

"Daughter, you have done nothing wrong. I know you were betrayed."

Betrayed. The word sunk like a knife into her chest.

The gentle voice continued. "They're only thinking about power and lust—they're not concerned about how they're hurting a little child. But now it's time to forgive them. You can release it to Me."

"But how can I forgive them? How can I release it to You? I've been betrayed by my own father." Hatred seethed in her heart like a boiling volcano ready to explode.

"Daughter, the only one who can judge this is Me. I am the only one who can fully understand. You must let Me have them, especially your father."

"But why did he do this?"

"Daughter, that answer will come later, but for now will you let go of this great debt he owes you? Will you trust Me to deal justly with the wrongdoer?"

"Yes," came the weak answer.

Jesus gently entwined His fingers with hers, and hand in hand they forgave the debt.

His own scarred wound pressed into Callie's pain. All the hate vanished like a vapor.

Slowly Callie's consciousness acclimated again to the reality of the counseling office.

"You OK?" Mike asked.

"Yeah. Yeah, I think so. Wow. I didn't die."

"No, you didn't die." Mike finally leaned back in his chair. He heaved a huge sigh as a smiled etched his face. "Go home and get some rest. That took a lot of you." He paused. "We'll meet again next week, and see how things have settled."

Callie nodded. As she walked out, she heard a song resounding through the building. Again she heard the words from the song "Friend of a Wounded Heart."

He did that, she thought. *He met me where I was. He's healing my wounded heart.*

Slowly, Callie tip-toed down the hall so she could see where the music was coming from. Peeking through the crack in the double doors, she saw a woman dancing and singing.

She's dancing my freedom.

At least, the beginning of it.

CHAPTER 7

The Choice

(Summer 1988)

Slavery comes in different forms. Callie had been sold into a different kind of slavery.

Mike's office had moved to a new church that met in a warehouse. Gravel crunched under the wheels of her minivan as she pulled up to the looming steel structure. Reluctantly, she entered the swinging glass doors at the front.

I guess they keep the lights out to save money. Dim emergency lights lit her navigation through the silent maze of hallways. She glanced into one empty classroom after another. *Is there something behind that door? My heart feels like it's going to jump out of my body.*

Finally she pulled a door open to see the brightly lit church office. And there was Mike, smiling at her from beside the receptionist desk.

"Come on in, and have a seat. How have things been since the last time we met?"

"Not so good." Callie sank down into the chair he offered and glared at the floor. "Every time I come here, I feel like I'm going to lose it."

Mike smiled slightly. "My friend, most people who come in here have stones in the road that need to be removed. You have boulders."

"Is that supposed to make me feel better?" She darted a glance up at him.

Mike explained again the process of healing Callie was in, but all she heard was muddled words. As her vision began to blur, her mind felt like a hornets' nest that had been disturbed by a child foolishly poking it with a stick. Angry hornets flying everywhere. Buzzing, buzzing. Ready to sting.

Breathe deeply, Callie. You'll be safe. I'm here. The voice came from deep within her this time.

Closing her eyes, she attempted to calm the violent voices screaming at her. Willfully, she forced the words. "Jesus, show me where this pain is coming from. I just want to be free."

You can't see this. You will die. Did these words come from herself or from an enemy?

"Remember, you didn't die. You lived. You can do this, with Jesus' help." Mike's soothing words convinced her mind to relent.

She closed her eyes and allowed her mind to drift back again. The seal on the next chapter cracked open.

"Oh, God," she cried. Instantaneously she saw herself as a four-year-old, tied to a table, thrashing, clawing at ropes that held her body fastened.

Child-like shrieks pierced her ears but then stopped. They seemed to have come from somewhere close to her.

A hooded man approached her with a metal prod that looked like a larger version of her mother's piano tuning fork. Methodically, he placed the prod against her tender skin as if commencing a surgical procedure.

Electrical lightning whipped through her body. She convulsed on the table. Every nerve frayed. Wild screams. Searing pain.

Repeatedly, the veiled man assaulted his victim. Callie felt as if a hammer had been taken to a perfectly smooth mirror reflecting her image.

Again and again the impact exploded the mirror, shattering it into thousands of splintered shards. Her mind now lay in thousands of tiny pieces.

"Jesus!" she cried. Instantly, He stood by her side.

"What they did to you, they did to Me," he said, but Callie saw fierceness in His eyes. At first she thought the anger was towards her, but then she realized it was towards her enemy.

"I am not angry with you, little one. Callie, I hate the evil that did this to you. I hurt when you hurt." He lifted her from the table, but she cringed at His touch, wiggling from His embrace.

"I understand why you don't trust Me, child, but I won't hurt you," Jesus reassured the shattered child pulling away from His loving arms.

Slowly the intensity of the moment lifted.

Through melted mascara, Callie glared at Mike. "I'm shattered." Anger seethed in her words. "How can He ever put back the pieces back together? I'm permanently damaged goods."

Mike leaned in from across the desk. "He can put the pieces back together. Callie, I know He can."

ಬಚ

That evening, Beth and Star snuggled up to their mama on the sofa while Alaia pulled herself up by the coffee table, diaper sagging. "Mama, play dress up." Beth grinned and rushed to get the tiara and cape. In a second, the two sisters marched in to perform their show, with the caboose of Alaia at the end.

"Look at this." "Watch me." Callie couldn't help but smile.

After the children had been tucked in and nighttime prayers prayed, Greg slipped into bed beside Callie. But she missed the obvious hopeful glance.

"Greg, all I feel is overwhelmed. Mike said what happened to me was something that happens to victims of satanic ritual abuse. They were intentionally trying to split my mind into parts so I wouldn't be able to remember what happened to me." She aimlessly picked at the bedspread. "It all seemed so surreal. I felt completely out of control. I could feel the electrical current pulsing through my body, but emotionally I was numb." Then Callie turned her tear-filled eyes to meet Greg's hopeful ones. "I'm scared. What if I do lose it? What will happen to you and the girls?"

Greg reached his arm around Callie, but she pulled away, hugging her pillow instead. "I feel like damaged goods. Why did you even marry me?" She wept into her pillow instead of Greg's willing shoulder.

Greg leaned over to breach the wall anyway. "Because I love you, sweetheart," he whispered.

A flash of her wedding night lit her mind. *Was I even a virgin, like I claimed? Was I just trying to make myself believe I was?* She had pushed the shame down, far away, but now the infection oozed out, affecting every area of their lives.

Callie languished to believe Greg's words of love, but they seemed unbelievable.

If only Mike were here. He could fix me.

ഔൠ

Precariously Callie drove to her next counseling appointment, absentminded, as if someone else were driving altogether. *Why do my hands and feet feel like ice cubes while my face feels like I have a fever?*

Mike met her at the door, and Callie's heart pulsed in her neck. *At least the camera in his office is working this time.*

"How are you feeling, any better?" Mike began pleasantly.

"Not really. In fact, my mind feels completely scrambled. I can't even focus on anything."

"Hmm. It seems that you have a lot of protection mechanisms. You remember these are there because you felt you couldn't handle what happened to you as a child. These parts of you held the pieces of emotions and memories so you could live and function. This ability was actually a gift from God for you so you could survive. As Jesus heals the pain, you won't need the protection mechanisms any longer. God will heal your mind and bring all that back together."

Callie was beginning to understand how her mind had protected her. "It was a gift from God," she repeated after him.

But what was once a gift now felt like a curse, because she constantly seemed to be fighting herself.

"Jesus. Take me by the hand, and lead me where I need to go." The words came a little easier from her lips, but all she saw was a blank screen. With the next chapter yet to open, she vaguely heard a familiar voice again. *No. You will die. I will kill you.*

Callie wanted to hide under a blanket the way she did when she was a little girl. But hiding had never deterred any of her monsters in the dark.

Please, I want the pain to end. Was this a death wish?

"Callie, the only way to get this pain out is to let Jesus in," Mike said. "Will you let Him in?"

Her mind relaxed a bit, and she began to see herself back in the old church fellowship hall, with her hands tied in front of her on the table. *You are a living sacrifice.*

"But I've already seen this," she protested. "You told me once we dealt with something, it was finished, and I didn't need to see it again." A lump grew in her throat as she fought back a torrent of tears. *Will I never be free of this?*

"When a memory is really traumatic, you have to see it in pieces, as much as you can handle for the time. Jesus is gentle and knows how much you can handle. There must still be something here you need to know. Trust Him."

This time, a butcher knife lifted above her. The hand holding it—she knew it was her father's. From somewhere near her another child's blood-curling shriek charged the room, then silence.

Something deep inside told her that her childhood friend had not survived, the little girl she had played with at church and had never seen again. Her ashen face turned in the direction of the scream, as beads of sweat rolled down her pale, clammy skin. Shocked and trembling, she peered into her father's hooded face. His compassionless eyes bore into her through the dark holes.

"Sacrifices must be made."

He must hate me. I am worthless. I don't deserve to live. Her body began to feel light, ethereal, like she was being lifted. Her extremities grew cold, very cold. The feeling crept up her arms and legs as the numbness crawled towards her heart. Her breathing shallowed to barely a weak breath.

"I'm dying. I feel myself dying." Her voice trailed off into silence.

Mike shifted in his chair uneasily. "Where is Jesus, Callie?" he prodded, wiping sweat from his brow.

It seemed like an eternity before either of them spoke.

"Callie, please say something." Mike's concerned tone brought Callie back.

"I don't know." An eerie quietness descended on her.

Child, I will take you home now if you want. But if you choose to stay, even though there will be suffering, you will have a great reward.

Callie hovered somewhere between this world and the next, longing for the pain to be over. But something inside wanted to live. She had a glimpse of a family, a whole family. She saw Mama's face.

"I will stay, Jesus."

Immediately, she was back in the office.

Carefully she tried to explain to Mike what she had heard and seen. The color came back into both of their faces.

She had chosen life. Mike smiled with relief.

Callie smiled back.

ꙮ

"Callie, I think you're getting too attached to Mike." Edith sat across from Callie at their regular diner, her typical straightforward manner causing Callie to squirm.

"But I need him. I mean, I can't do this without him." The true confession spilled out.

"You need Jesus, Callie. You're married to Greg. I think you need to be really careful here." Edith's tone was challenging. "After all, there's something called emotional adultery."

Callie looked down at her uneaten sandwich. "It will be fine," she said. But the word *adultery* stung.

"You should keep this in the light with Greg," Edith warned.

As Callie drove home, she clutched the steering wheel. "Do I really have to tell him, Lord? What if he hates me? What if he leaves me?"

But she knew what she had to do as soon as she got home.

"Hon, I need to talk to you," Callie's voice trembled.

"What happened with Edith?" Greg asked, following her into the bedroom and closing the door.

"Something she said really hit me hard." Callie sat down on the bed. "I think I'm growing too attached to Mike. I don't want to do anything wrong, but I feel like I need him so much right now. I've got to finish what I've started, at least until some relief comes." Her chest heaved from the shame that washed over her. "Please don't leave me." Tears washed her face.

Stunned, Greg stood motionless for a moment. His face grew red as tears gathered in his eyes. "Callie, I'm not sure what to say." He began to turn his back to her, but then suddenly stopped. As he turned to face her again, he threw his arms open wide. "Sweetheart, I should have been going with you. I've made you do this all alone, but that won't happen anymore."

A week later Greg sat fidgeting in the chair beside her, and yet his presence offered her some sense of strength and comfort. Somehow it felt like the fear lessened with him there.

Callie took a deep breath. "The panic attacks are still really strong," she said, "and I feel like I'm afraid of everything."

"Then you know what to do," Mike responded. "Let's ask Jesus to show you where this is coming from."

Callie trembled all over, but she felt Greg taking hold of her hand.

"Mike, are you sure this is the best thing to do?" Greg interrupted. "I mean this has been really hard on Callie. On our family," he hesitated.

"On you," Mike added. "Greg, I'm sure this has been very hard on you."

Mike looked from Greg to Callie. "I'm sure Callie has filled you in on how this works. She's told me that she's sharing everything with you. I know this is hard to look at. Hard to believe your wife has endured this, but from every indication, she has. Let's allow Jesus to show Callie where this is coming from, so she can heal." Greg nodded in agreement and eased back into his chair.

Mentally, Callie drifted back through time, as the next pages turned.

Stars blinked in a black sky. Faintly, the memory came into blurry view. Scents of burning human hair filled her nostrils. Flames blazing intermingled with the darkness. The smells combined with the heat felt suffocating.

Odd forms swayed in a demonic dance. Wolves peered out of the darkness, ready to devour their prey. A white, bitter powder was placed on her lips. Her head felt fuzzy, dizzy.

Mama grabbed her, shoving her towards the tornado shelter. Opening it, she placed Callie in the dirt hole. "Don't move or make a sound," her mother desperately whispered, putting a finger over her lips. The steel doors creaked shut.

Trembling, Callie obeyed. Her skin crawled at the thought of what was in the darkness with her. *Buried alive in a premature grave.* Shaken and terrified, she pressed her face against the cold metal.

Then, suddenly, she felt a strange warmth envelope her in the pit. She could not see him, but she knew it was her Lord. Through the cracks she could still see the dancing flames, but her heavy eyelids gave in to sleep as she rested, embraced in the Presence.

Suddenly her father came to fetch her, abruptly startling her awake. Dizzily spinning, she saw the hooded beings as they danced around the inferno. Round and round.

Like black sheep, dark figures were led to the slaughter. A cross burned in the distance. She sank to her knees beneath the heat and heaviness, vomiting.

"Callie, are you OK?" Greg squeezed her hand.

"Don't touch me! It hurts!"

Then Mike spoke. "Callie, where is Jesus in this memory?"

She tried to focus, but everything kept coming in and out of view. "Jesus, where are you?" Like a statue she sat frozen in the chair, trying to look at the memory.

In her mind, an image came up that at first looked like Jesus, but as he drew closer, Callie's stomach turned. This vile man proclaimed he was Jesus, but he began to touch Callie in her private places, making her squirm.

"No!" Her face contorted. She scrambled back to flee his presence, but she could not avoid his violating touch.

"Callie, that's just a man who claimed to be Jesus. He's lying to you," Mike said. "Ask for the true Lord Jesus."

Callie obeyed. Suddenly, light came from behind the man. She saw another figure coming forward, pushing the first out of the way. He was light and beautiful. His loving gaze penetrated through to Callie.

She felt ashamed, but His eyes were not condemning.

"Callie, come closer," He said. "Look at My hands and My feet. Do you see the pierced holes? I am love. Love never rapes. Love never takes. Love always gives. Look for these marks, Callie. You will know Me by My sacrificial love, by the scars in My hands and My feet."

Jesus reached out to her, arms open wide. This time she didn't hold back. She ran into His embrace.

As she wept, He cried with her, holding her close to His side.

"Callie, you must release these, even these to Me. You must forgive them, child. It's the only way to be free." His words soothed her raw heart.

With Jesus's arm wrapped around her, she and her Savior turned to forgive those who not only had damaged her life, but had destroyed the lives of others. How could she forgive such sin?

Only by the true love that washed through her from His presence.

The pages flipped open easier now. *Maybe this is the end of it?*

It was only the beginning.

Part 2

"I acknowledged my sin to You,
and my iniquity I did not hide.
I said, I will confess my transgressions to the Lord,
continually unfolding the past till all is told,
and then You instantly forgave me the guilt
and iniquity of my sin."
Psalm 32:5 (Amplified)

CHAPTER 8

Callie, age 4

St. Petersburg, Florida

Callie clung to Mama's skirt as Me-Ma ushered them through the open door into Mama's childhood home. Baby Eva nuzzled between Mama's breasts.

But Callie's father lingered outside, leaning against the mango tree at the entrance of the driveway, shifting his weight from one foot to the other uncomfortably.

"Well, come here, you little darling." Callie saw her grandpa squatting down with arms open wide to greet her. After a few minutes of doting on Callie, he looked up. "Well, look what the cat drug home," he said to Mama. "Looks like you've been eating well enough." Mama lowered her head and stared at the carpet as her face grew red.

Grandma knew how to ease the tension. "Cheryl, Pastor knows you're back and asked if you would sing in church on Sunday. It would be like when you were a young girl. You have the voice of an angel, sweetheart."

"The voice of an angel," Mama mockingly muttered to herself. But she hesitantly agreed as Callie danced around her feet. Callie loved when her Mama sang. Truly, it was the sweetest sound she had heard. "Oh, Mama's gonna sing like an angel!"

On Sunday Callie went with her family to the church where Mama had grown up. As she entered the auditorium holding tightly to Me-Ma's gloved hand, Callie stood for a moment stunned by the grand white room with polished wooden pews.

On cue, Mama took the stage and sang in perfect tones, "The Old Rugged Cross." A broad smile spread across Callie's face as she gleamed with pride. *Is Mama really an angel?*

Then the preacher acknowledged her father. "Warren, please come up and greet the congregation."

Proudly, her father took his place behind the pulpit. "Praise be to God. . . ."

His words melted away as Callie fidgeted in her seat, thinking of the chocolate cake Me-Ma had baked that morning, and only a pinch from Mama made her straighten up.

Afterwards, the friends of the family crowded around her parents to welcome Mama back to town and admire the two babies. Some men caught her father in a hearty handshake or two.

Then, unexpectedly, he swung around and took Callie's hand from Me-Ma. Patting it, he announced, "And this is my eldest daughter, Callie."

For some reason the chuckles of her father's friends seemed unnerving to Callie, and she couldn't wait to get away, back to her grandparents' home.

Later that afternoon, when Callie was helping Me-Ma set the table for dinner, she asked, "Me-Ma, do we get to live here with you forever?"

"No, dear," Me-Ma sighed. "Your father has already taken on a small church across town. You'll be moving into the parsonage day after tomorrow."

Callie's lip quivered, and tears pricked her eyes. But she quickly wiped them off with the back of her hand before Me-Ma could see.

Move they did, to the middle of the metropolis in the downtown district. Every street was mapped carefully into exact blocks. Traffic zipped in and out. Callie had never seen so many cars in her life. Or people. People swarmed everywhere like flies on a pile of poop.

Sandy ground replaced the Texas baked clay. Eerie moss hung from the trees and power lines. Hurricanes replaced tornadoes. Palms trees lined the boulevards, swaying with coconuts tucked in their boughs.

This time "church" would be held in the cement block building next to the simple parsonage, but Sunday school would be taught in their home. The house and small church sat next to the underside of a highway overpass, covered with neon graffiti. The constant clamor of cars passing overhead, horns honking, tires screeching, and sirens blaring soon blended into the ordinary background noise of life.

✂

Rocking on the tiled floor of the Floridian home, Callie snuggled in the arms of her Me-Ma. *I'm safe here.*

Me-Ma was an immaculate housekeeper and a wonderful cook. She did everything she could to please her husband.

Before he came home from the shipyard each day, she was sure to shower, fix her hair, and put on fresh makeup. "What are you doing, Me-Ma?" Callie questioned, watching Me-Ma meticulously apply her lip rouge with their reflection in the mirror of the cedar vanity.

"Gotta make sure your Paw-Paw wants to come home every night." Me-Ma took Callie by the hand and announced, "Let's go put dinner on the table."

Tall etched glasses, porcelain plates, and flatware were put in their proper place setting as Me-Ma insisted. A bouquet of purple hydrangea from her flourishing garden served as the centerpiece.

Suddenly, a rush of love and admiration filled Callie's heart. "This is so beautiful. I love you, Me-Ma. I wish I could stay here forever."

Me-Ma came close, hugging Callie to her side. "I love you too, sweetheart."

That evening after supper, Callie toddled on Paw-Paw's knee as he bounced her in the air. "You are my sunshine," [*] he sang to her. She loved hearing it.

His thick, deep voice echoed as it bounced off the solid block walls. Those walls were built for any storm.

☙ℰ❧

Callie's father's parents lived close by as well, in a clammy block house. Everything in that house, it seemed, was colored puke green, even down to every purse in Grandmother's closet.

---

[*] Oliver Hood or Paul Rice (disputed), "You Are My Sunshine." Recorded by Paul Rice, Decca Records, 1939.

At their house, as Callie sat watching TV she could see her father's childhood bedroom. For some reason she wanted to avoid it like a haunted mansion. And in the room across from that, Callie wondered what her uncle spent all those hours doing, with his heavy curtains drawn.

When he was home, her undertaker grandfather sat in his puke-green easy chair with a grim look on his pale face. "Your father was raised above the funeral home," he often told her in his ghostly voice.

Callie didn't even understand what a funeral home was like. She shivered, thinking of a puke-green room where dead bodies were laid out, row upon row.

But there did come a day when she found out what the funeral home was like. That was the day her father and grandfather took her there for a visit.

CHAPTER 9

Unraveling

(Late Summer 1988)

Callie twisted the hem of her t-shirt into a knot as Greg pulled into this unfamiliar parking lot. She felt nauseated by the August heat.

Mike, whom she had finally come to trust, was gone. It just didn't make sense.

And now here they were, starting all over with a new man, whose military bearing intimidated her.

So Raymond's large grin and congenial manner surprised her. "Callie, it's so good to meet you, and Greg. Please, please sit down."

Hmmm. He seems "fatherly," but I can't trust a father.

"I've looked over your notes," Raymond began, "and it seems you've already dealt with a lot with Mike. I know his dismissal must have been alarming to you, and I understand if you don't trust me."

Maybe I should ask him about Mike. But what good would it do?

Instead, Greg began. "Well, we've heard good things about you from our pastor. Where does Callie go from here?"

Raymond nodded thoughtfully. "Much of what I believe about inner healing is based on Matthew 18," he said. "I believe that the servant who didn't forgive from his heart his fellow servant the small debt after he had been forgiven so much, represents what happens to us when we haven't forgiven from our heart."

Callie crossed her arms as Raymond continued.

"From what I understand, the 'heart' is where memories are stored. Our first-time memories are like a blueprint for our lives, affecting the rest of our lives. They tell our hearts how to act and respond to the world around us, because this is the first record of how we should feel, think, and so forth.

"But when we're children, we often don't know how to deal with our emotions when we're hurt, which means that many times we'll believe lies about what we're feeling. Because of this, the enemy can gain an open door to torture us in our thoughts or our emotions. If we ask Jesus to take us to the root, and the healing happens from there, then we can walk out of prison, so to speak."

Raymond leaned forward. "Young lady, based on what I see in you now, and what I've read in your notes, you're still being tortured by emotions you don't want to feel and by lies you've believed. I want to see you come into more of who God really created you to be."

But Callie still sat with her arms crossed. She had gotten stuck back at almost his first sentence. "Are you saying the things that happened to me were small debts?"

Raymond paused. "Callie, the things that happened to you were horrendous, and should never have been done to anyone, much less a little girl." His voice cracked, he adjusted his glasses, and Callie thought she saw his eyes glistening.

He cleared his throat and continued. "I know you made some progress with Mike, and I'm proud of you for that, but are you ready to continue the process? Are you ready to ask the true Lord Jesus where these things are coming from? And most important, will you trust me to help you?"

I can't trust anyone. And I'm not about to let my guard down.

But what choice do I have?

Then she heard another voice, coming from within.

Callie, I always give you a choice. You don't have to do this, but if you will trust Me in this, you will find who you really are, and who I really am.

A response welled up. *I'm not sure I want to know.*

Raymond interrupted her thoughts. "Callie, are you ready to start?"

The storm inside that had abated in the past few weeks was swirling up again. But desperation led her to action.

She sighed. "OK. I'll try." Her right leg violently shook as she closed her eyes, and she allowed herself to begin seeing again.

Suddenly her mind ranted. *You can't trust him!* A death grip tightened around her neck.

"Are you seeing something, Callie?" Raymond asked.

"No." Callie gripped her leg, willing it to stop shaking.

"What would happen if you allowed yourself to see something?" Raymond pressed.

"Death," she whispered.

But Raymond was undeterred, speaking with gentle, soothing words she had heard before. "You know that you already lived through it, because you're here with Greg and me. You can let Jesus into the memory, and He can help you."

The book cover creaked open, and the pages began flipping, as it fell open to the next sealed chapter.

Callie saw her father and grandfather tightly grasping her hands on either side as they entered the mortuary. The stench of formaldehyde sickened her stomach, and she gagged.

They continued to walk her into a room lined with caskets, some opened, some closed. Callie struggled to free her hands, but their fingernails dug into her wrists.

All at once, Callie's father stopped, demanding she stand still. Then he stripped her of her cotton summer dress as her grandfather opened the casket lined with red velvet.

"Put her in here," her grandfather ordered. Father obeyed, forcing Callie inside the casket.

The lid shut down with an echoed thud. Terrified, she lay like a corpse in the silence.

"Please, let me out! I'll do anything!" She clawed at the coffin lid, trying to push it open. "Please, don't let me die!"

But her efforts were futile.

Raymond's voice broke through the terrifying memory. "Callie, you can ask Jesus where He is."

"Jesus, please help me." Callie's voice felt small and far away.

Threads of light seeped around the edge of the casket lid. Then suddenly the top burst open. The brightness blinded her eyes for a moment.

Then she saw Him. Jesus was there, lifting her out and holding her. For a moment, she felt embraced in perfect love.

But then as she felt His touch, her body stiffened. She was painfully aware of her nakedness in His arms and could easily imagine the ways He would violate her.

But His eyes . . . she gazed into His eyes and knew He would love her and protect her.

Raymond's voice came again from someplace far away. "Callie, what they did was wrong and never should have been done to you. But you can let Jesus have them now."

"But why did they do this to me? They must hate me." Tears welled in her eyes. "I'm worthless."

"No, Callie." This time the rich voice came from the One she saw holding her. "They were trying to terrify you so they could control you and make you do whatever they wanted you to do. This was their sin, not yours." He paused and looked her right in the eyes. "Daughter, your father was treated this same way as a child, as was your grandfather. Sometimes people who have been hurt choose to hurt others." Jesus' eyes were full of tenderness. "But you can release them to Me, My daughter. I know how to judge them, completely and rightly, for what they have done."

Streams of tears ran down her hot cheeks as she spoke the words again. "Dad, I forgive you for what you did. For terrifying me." Lightness filled her heart, and her leg stopped shaking. But her head throbbed, and she ached all over.

"Are you ready to continue?" Raymond asked.

Why do I have to dig up all these dead bones? But in spite of herself, Callie nodded. Her leg began shaking violently again. As Callie asked Jesus to show her the next memory, the whole sofa began to feel as if an earthquake had hit.

Across the screen of her mind zipped a flash of her father's face. Then a picture began to emerge. They were driving up to Me-Ma and Paw-Paw's church. It wasn't Sunday, and only a few cars dotted the parking lot. In her gut, Callie knew something terrible was about to happen.

Her father turned the key in a door and led her down the long hallway of Sunday school rooms. They turned into one of the rooms, where a few nicely-dressed men greeted her father.

"I told the pastor we're having a prayer meeting."

She could hear the snickers as her father spoke.

Callie's father pointed to a jar on the table. "She goes to the highest bidder."

In Raymond's office on the sofa, Callie jerked out of that memory. "O God," she exclaimed as she sank into a fetal position. Shame overtook her from a deep sense of betrayal. She wanted to fight, to kick, to bite, but she knew it was futile.

"What's going on, Callie?" It was Greg's strained voice this time.

Her voice cracked. "I've been sold." She grabbed Greg's hand.

This time he too joined in the grieving, the anger, and finally, the prayers of forgiveness and release.

"Callie, what these men did was wrong," Raymond said gently. "How they treated you was wicked. Forgiving them does not excuse their sin."

"I know, but I feel like a piece of trash," she muttered.

"If I throw a diamond in the pig sty and stomp on it, does it become something different than a diamond? Does its value change?"

"I guess not." She tried to look at him, but everything was blurry through her swollen eyes.

"Well, my dear friend, no matter what these men did to try to soil you or damage you, they could never change your intrinsic value. You're still worth a million dollars. Nothing anyone ever does can change that."

The voices inside Callie started talking in her head again.

What if what he's saying is true?

He's only saying that because he wants to take from you what every man wants to take.

Yeah, it's not safe to trust. Anyone. Ever.

ʀʊʊʒ

Edith wanted to meet with her again.

Ever since the last meeting with Raymond, Callie had been tired to the depths of her soul. She struggled with wondering if her children would be safer without her. How could she even express to Edith the darkness she felt inside?

Edith shook her head in disapproval. "I don't understand why you keep doing this to yourself, Callie. Ever since you started going through this counseling stuff, you've changed."

The statement stung. She wasn't sure how she got up the courage to speak. "Sometimes I feel like you put me under a microscope."

"Maybe I do."

A chill swept between them.

Callie didn't want to lose her friend, but she gathered up her courage to continue. "Have you ever read *The Voyage of the Dawn Treader* by C.S. Lewis?"

"Yes, but it's been years. Why?"

"Well, there's a part where Eustace finds a golden band on an island. He slips it on his arm and becomes a hideous dragon, and he can't do anything to change himself back."

"What does that have to do with anything?"

"I feel like that hideous dragon."

Edith paused, eying Callie up and down. "But he doesn't stay that way, does he?"

"No, you're right. Aslan finds him at the end." Callie hesitantly clawed at the air to imitate the great lion. "He rips off all the layers of dragon scales and dragon flesh, until all that's left is Eustace standing there, you know, naked. And vulnerable. Then Aslan washes off the rest of the dragon slime and dresses him in new clothes."

Edith raised an eyebrow to indicate that she was ready for Callie to get to the point.

Callie hesitated and stammered. "A-and after that, Eustace is a new boy." She took a deep breath and spoke quickly. "And that's what I feel like God is doing to me, like He's ripping dragon flesh off. I just wonder what the little girl inside will look like when He's done. It feels so incredibly vulnerable. And I'm afraid of what I'll find."

ᔥᔥ

As Callie arrived home later than normal, she opened the door to find Greg holding baby Alaia in his arms. "Honey, she's sick."

Callie saw the weak look in Alaia's red eyes and immediately called the doctor.

"They want us to watch her through the night and bring her in the morning." The little baby's sweaty brow and labored breathing stirred something inside Callie, causing her to press her palms against her eyes.

All night Callie slept next to Alaia, like a watchman on the wall, every hour slipping a thermometer under her sweaty arm, listening to the familiar sound of wheezing slipping in and out of Alaia cracked lips.

"Mama"—sucking air—"help me."

That didn't come from Alaia—she was only nine months old. Callie jolted up in the dim light of the nursery.

"Warren. We have to get her to the hospital. We have no choice."

Warren? That was Callie's own father. She pressed her palms to her eyes.

Breathe. Just breathe, Callie.

Blurred vision. Darkness. Mama sitting beside me in the back of the car.

"Pneumonia again?" She heard her father's voice, harsh, sarcastic.

Callie put her hand to her chest and took a deep breath. Flashes of her own childhood pneumonia raced through her mind.

Morning, please come quickly.

Seven times. Seven times the year she was three. She knew, because she heard her father's voice saying it.

Morning finally came, and Callie hurried to dress them both.

"Callie, you'll have to do this yourself." Greg stood in the doorway. "I've got to go to work."

"We can't afford this again!" Her father cursed as he drove the old station wagon to the hospital. *"I have bills to pay!"*

Callie carefully buckled a listless Alaia into her car seat. *She must feel really bad. She's too tired to cry. O God. Help my baby.*

"Mama"—wheezing breath—"help me."

The doctor confirmed Callie's fears. "If we treat this pneumonia now, we can avoid the hospital."

The hospital.

Somehow gazing beyond the pert young nurse dressed in Scooby Doo scrubs, Callie saw a blur of frantic emergency personnel, white coats, blinding lights, and sirens, all muddled together. She tightly held Alaia, who was lying limp, wheezing, trying to get a full breath.

Please, God, please heal my baby.

The nurse in the Scooby Doo scrubs pricked Alaia's finger, squeezing out the blood until the tiny finger looked like it would pop. Callie felt suddenly nauseated, squeezed her eyes shut, and turned her head away.

There was the white, cloudy world of an oxygen tent, with strangers all around.

So tired. So tired.

Callie shook herself and willed her eyes back open to focus on Alaia.

I'm so scared. God, are you punishing me? Why couldn't Greg have come? He didn't want to take care of our daughter, and I can't. Callie began to tremble.

Finally, as the last trickle of blood slipped into the glass tube, the nurse stroked Callie's arm. "She'll be fine. Don't worry. We'll send you home with a machine that will help her breathe."

Callie let out a deep sigh.

There was Tucker's face. *"I have a friend to keep you company in the hospital."* Callie reached for the sock monkey and smiled, holding it close to her heart.

CHAPTER 10

Callie, age 7

All over Florida

"Callie, go see what your sister is up to," Mama called. "She's too quiet."

Obediently, Callie went to the bedroom she shared with Eva. Sure enough, her three-year-old sister had found Mama's lipstick. Eva smiled broadly with delight, showing giant fuchsia lips and teeth smudged with fuchsia. Then she pointed to the fuchsia squiggles on the carpet.

"Oh no!" Callie blurted out. "Mama's gonna be so mad!" She scrambled to start cleaning up, but Mama came before she was able to finish.

"What are you girls—" Mama gasped. "Oh, that will never come out of the carpet. Callie Mae. Get over here now." Mama smacked her cheek hard. "I told you watch your sister."

The words stung more than the slap.

"But Mama, I tried," Callie whimpered. *It's always my fault.*

That night in bed, Callie heard her parents' voices in the next room. "Damn it, Cheryl. I don't have the money for another mouth to feed." Voices muffled as she heard Mama's sobs.

Too many mouths. Too many mouths. Callie pulled the sheet firmly over her head.

The next day, Callie heard Mama groaning in the bathroom. "What's wrong, Mama?" she asked, peeking around the slightly-open door.

With a look of horror on her ashen face, Mama quickly slammed the door. Somehow Callie knew she had been trying to get rid of the need for more money. *Too many mouths.*

Her brother was born five months later anyway. An Easter gift. Daniel Adam. A little man in a lion's den.

ༀ

Callie peered out the window of her "other grandparents'" car. They were going for their Sunday afternoon drive while Mama was in the hospital with little Daniel.

Suddenly Callie heard her grandfather's gruff voice mutter, "Nigger town."

She saw that the streets were lined with run-down buildings, boards haphazardly nailed over their broken windows. Graffiti obscenities were sprayed on the walls.

"What's a nigger?" Callie asked.

When they stopped at a light, she saw a black man shuffle across the crosswalk with his hands pushed down into his pockets. He turned and faced the direction of their car, a despondent look in his eyes.

"It's a person with black skin, Callie." Grandmother's voice was tight, strained.

Callie didn't understand her grandfather's disgust. After all, she had just met a little girl with dark skin at school that past week. They were both alone, so Callie had sat across from her at the lunch table. The girl with woven pig tails had smiled a pleasant grin. The two had hit it off immediately, and their friendship grew daily. Her first true friendship was blossoming.

What's wrong with having black skin? She kept her thoughts to herself, not voicing them aloud, so as not to agitate Grandfather.

❧☙

One day Me-Ma and Paw-Paw told Callie they were going to go visit the resting place of her great-grandma. After driving through an ancient looking stone archway, Callie saw moss-covered tombstones with worn inscriptions dotting the landscape. Here and there she saw fresh dirt dug up in rectangles. Holding tightly to Paw-Paw and Me-Ma's hands, she tipped-toed through the headstones to the place where her great-grandma's remains were laid.

"Be careful, Callie," Me-Ma warned. "Don't step on a grave. It's bad luck."

Bad luck indeed. Just that past week her father had given a fiery sermon about hell fire for those who dishonored their elders. His words rang in her ears. "To repent of your sins, you have to dress in sackcloth and ashes and cry out for forgiveness. If you don't, you will surely burn in hell."

"Careful, Callie, careful," she repeated out loud to herself. "If you step on a grave it will dishonor the dead."

As Me-Ma bent over to place a handful of daisies on Great-grandma's grave, Callie's attention was suddenly diverted by a beautiful butterfly. As she turned to look, her legs lost their balance. She stumbled back to catch herself, but stepped directly onto a freshly-dug grave.

Callie's face flushed hot, and she felt like she was going to be sick. Her ears buzzed so loudly that she could barely hear Me-Ma saying, "What are you doing, Callie? You're not supposed to step there!"

In the weeks that followed, everywhere Callie went with her family she looked for ashtrays. She needed to find one that had the enough residue that she could collect it to put on her head. The next time Mama bought potatoes she would snatch the burlap sack. Then, with sackcloth and ashes, she would weep and wail for forgiveness. Otherwise she knew she would be eternally damned.

The next Sunday morning after Sunday school, for some reason, Mama turned to Callie and said, "Callie, do you want to give your heart to Jesus?"

Callie had learned that life worked best when she showed no emotion at all, but this time she couldn't help it. Like a bubble bursting, her body began to shake. "I can't, Mama," she blurted out. "I'm going to hell."

Mama's eyes widened in a look of astonishment. "What do you mean?"

The story tumbled pitifully out of Callie's mouth.

"Sweetheart, you misunderstood what your father was saying. He was talking about the city of Nineveh, the one in the Old Testament. That's not true for today. All you have to do is say the sinner's prayer, believe it, and you'll be saved."

Hope sprang up in Callie's heart. "Yes, Mama. Can we pray that now?" Together they bowed their heads and recited the words.

Mama smiled. "Now, you have to go down front of the church to make it official at the altar call next Sunday. You have to profess your decision to follow Jesus to the church. And then you have to be baptized."

Just relieved not to have to wear a brown sack and ashes, Callie agreed.

The following Sunday, her heart raced while the organ played "I Surrender All." Callie walked the carpeted aisle, the path of many a sinner, to proclaim her faith. At the front she was met by the pastor—her father. He appeared to pride himself in his daughter's decision. Afterwards, friends patted him on the back.

A week later, her father stood in the waist-deep waters of the baptismal, took her by the hands, and religiously recited, "In the name of the Father, the Son, and the Holy Spirit, I baptize you." He placed his hand over her mouth and lowered her under the water. "Buried in the likeness of His death," he said. Then he pulled her back up. "Raised in the likeness of His resurrection."

೮ාඏ

"What do you think you're doing, you stupid brats?" the bully barked. Eva and Daniel, who had been innocently playing in their backyard, stopped in their tracks and looked up at the smirking four-foot giant. He stood like a miniature Goliath on the other side of the back fence and continued to hurl insults and taunts. Eva began to cry, holding Daniel close to her side. Callie's new puppy, Terrance, yipped protectively at the edge of the fence.

Callie was sick of bullies. She had encountered bullies at every new school she had entered here in Florida, and she was sick of them. She had to intervene and scare him off, to defend her helpless siblings.

Grabbing a huge rock, she heaved it over the fence.

It hit its mark directly on top of Goliath's head. The boy staggered and fell backwards on the ground stunned.

But she hadn't meant to actually hit him—she only wanted to scare him.

"Oh, you killed him!" Daniel exclaimed with victorious excitement.

But the victim's mother had seen the entire crime. "You'll pay for this!" she yelled, as she helped her son stumble back across the street.

That night in the back bedroom, Callie's father seethed, "How could you embarrass us like that?" He stripped her shorts and panties down to her knees. He unbuckled his belt, yanking it from around his waist so fast that it zinged in the air. "I'll teach you never to embarrass our family again."

Vengeance was his. He was good to his word. For two days following the torture, the red welts blazed on her legs and Callie winced every time she moved on her bed.

For a week she was banished to her room, the week before Christmas. The only reason Father finally let her out was that they were going to Me-Ma's and Paw-Paw's for the holiday.

The holiday . . .

Everything was perfect for Christmas.

Mama's voice sounded cheerful as she called for the children to get on their best clothes and get into the car.

Her grandparents' home was an amazing bazaar of brightly colored bulbs on the tinseled tree, smells of honey ham baking in the stove, and joy-filled merriment.

Callie had just been shut into her room for a week. Now they were the happy, godly family.

This was Callie's normal.

Over Christmas dinner, Mama meekly announced one more Christmas surprise. "I'm pregnant with our fourth."

Me-Ma clapped for joy, but Father abruptly left the table.

Six months later, Lita was born.

෴

Callie came home from the last day of school that year to find boxes all over the place.

Moving boxes again. She stood in the middle of the room just staring at them. *Where to this time?*

The whole time they'd been in Florida, her father had floated from church to part-time job to business scheme to church again. Since moving to Florida, they had moved all across the long state from St. Petersburg to the Keys to Jacksonville to Sarasota.

Callie had lost count of how many different elementary schools she had attended, every time having to be the "new girl." Every time needing to learn the rules of that place, every time having to figure out who was the bully she needed to avoid. Moving so many times, she sometimes didn't even get to say good-bye to any new friends she might have made. Moving so often that she often didn't even get a chance to make friends.

"This time we're leaving the state." Her father answered the question she hadn't asked. "We aren't coming back."

His voice had a ring of finality to it.

"Where are we going this time?" Callie's words held an edge of defiance.

"Your father wants to move north," Mama said. She set her mouth firmly, leaning over her belly growing with the fourth new life, and grabbed a box to start loading books into it. "It won't be so bad. You'll see."

"But Mama, what about Me-Ma and Paw-Paw? We won't be able to see them if we move that far." In the awkward silence that followed, Callie looked from one parent to the other, trying to read them. She saw Mama's set jaw and averted eyes as she busily packed the books. She saw Father's glare as he sat doing nothing.

Then suddenly she knew. *He doesn't want me here with them. He wants to take me away from them.*

Callie's heart pounded as her anger rose. "I want to stay here, with them."

This is when Mama finally shot her a "look."

Silent. Keep silent.

Something raged on Callie's insides. Something she didn't even know how to identify, since she didn't know words like *grief, bitterness*, and *shame*.

But she had been used to shutting down her emotions when they accidentally started to show. So once again she slammed the iron door to her heart with a deafening thud, as she had so often had to do to survive. She bit into her knuckle hard, leaving imprints of white.

CHAPTER 11

The Hatchet

(Winter 1989)

On the outside, their family seemed completely normal. Peaceful. Happy. Fully functional.

Peaceful and happy. That's what "shut down and numb" looks like to everybody else.

Chaotic and full of turmoil, but you don't see it. I'm just getting dragon flesh ripped off of me, that's all. I don't know what will be left at the end, but no worries.

Read this book, they said. So Callie did.

Pray this prayer, they said. So Callie did.

Go through this class, they said. So Callie did.

Memorize these Scriptures, tape them to your bathroom mirror, say them ten times a day.

So Callie did.

Sometimes it would help, for a while. But the moment she let down her guard, she was right back in the chaotic numbness. Or maybe it was numb chaos. The swirling spiraling anxiety that made her feel like she was going to snap at any second.

But not at church. At church everything was always, "Just great, and you?"

She hated it. She wished she didn't have to go, but Greg kept insisting.

"You have such beautiful, sweet girls." An elderly woman stopped her in the hall and touched Alaina's little hand.

Callie smiled and murmured a humble reply as Star began barking and panting. "Oh, haha. She likes to pretend she's a dog."

"Well, that's just adorable." The old woman chuckled. "You are truly blessed."

After dropping her girls off in the children's rooms, Callie made her way back to Greg, who had again saved her a seat in the middle of the pew near the front instead of at the end in the back where she *needed* to sit. *Why does he keep doing that?*

If I can't sit in the back on the end, it will probably take me a full five seconds per person to climb out and an extra ten seconds to get to the door. Which exit is closer when I sit here? If I crashed through that window, would it be worth all the broken glass?

Every week her church daydreams ran along similar lines.

ఴఙ

Finally they were home and back in the normal chaos of life. Dinner was finished and Callie was cleaning up when she suddenly stopped and felt the blood rush from her face.

What is wrong with me? She grabbed the edge of the counter. *Why does seeing a knife in the sink make me have a vision of a knife in my hand to kill someone?*

"O Jesus!" she repeated over and over, "I don't want to hurt my children. I don't want to hurt my children."

As the raucous tunes of *Sesame Street* played in the next room, she backed out of the kitchen.

The phone rang. "Hello?" Her voice sounded too high. "Oh, hi Mom. Oh, I'm OK." She paused at a question. "Well, I'm in the closet." Her voice quavered.

"Why are you in the closet, Callie? Where are the girls?" She heard the concern in her mom's voice . . . and something else.

Callie hesitated to answer—letting her mom know her true feelings could be dangerous.

But against her better judgment, she decided to plunge.

"I'm afraid I might hurt them."

Her mom's high-pitched voice shot back, with words like arrows zinging through the air towards their target. "You sound like one of those people on the news who kill their kids! You need to get some help!"

The words sunk into Callie's heart like a hatchet buried deep in her flesh. *Bull's eye mark hit.*

Thanks, Mom.

ဆဝ၆ဒ

A week later, Callie sat beside Greg and in front of Raymond, rocking back and forth, trying to calm her racing thoughts.

"My mom thinks I might hurt my kids. Am I going to lose my mind?"

"Callie, I've dealt with people who are criminals, remember? You are not a murderer. You're not going to hurt your children. Have you ever done anything to hurt them up to this point?"

"Well, no. But sometimes I feel so out of control. When the panic hits, my head feels like it's spinning, and it's so hard to concentrate."

"That's how anxiety makes you feel. But it doesn't mean you'll lose your mind. Your mind is an amazing gift, and it helps to protect you and others from harm. You're here because you want to get help, because you want to do what's right. If you had any intention of hurting anyone you wouldn't be sitting here with me."

"I guess you're right," she slowly agreed. But the lie had sunk deep and hooked onto other things buried within her.

If you tell anyone, I'll destroy you and your family. There was one of the old familiar lies ringing through her mind.

She wanted to be done with keeping secrets. But could the dragon destroy her family for finally "telling"?

"Close your eyes, Callie, and we can follow the true Lord Jesus to what you need to see today to pursue freedom."

"But why is this whole process taking so long to get through?" Callie was stalling.

"Because you were a very hurt and wounded little girl." Raymond sounded fatherly. "Now let's see where this takes us."

Callie finally nodded and closed her eyes. "Jesus, show me where You want me to go."

A dark outline of pine trees came into view silhouetted against the starlit sky. Angry shouts echoed, then a loud shattering of glass. Smoke filled Callie's lungs, and she choked.

Blazing flames shot through the windows of a farmhouse in the distance, lighting up the night. Callie could hear screams, but the cloaked crowd standing outside did not move to intervene. A cross engulfed in flames stood beside the blaze. The smell, the heat, the sight caused her to wretch. There in the clearing, she began to vomit.

Greg and Raymond saw her face turn deathly pale and her body stiffen.

"Callie, what's happening?" Raymond's voice called her back to reality. "Where's Jesus?"

Callie tried to find words, but the numbness overtook her. It all seemed surreal. Bewildered, she asked, "Am I making all this up?"

"No, Callie," Raymond said. "Even if you could make up the events, you can't make up these emotions. Your perception may have been different, because you were a child, but I do believe you're remembering true events." Then he added, "Can you release this crime to the Lord? Can you let go and forgive them?"

Callie nodded mutely, still at a loss for words. Raymond led it this time.

"Are you ready to ask Jesus what else He wants you to see?"

Again Callie nodded mutely.

Again, her legs began to shake. Leaning back in the recliner, she drifted to another place, her father's parents' house, floating in like a ghost haunting familiar territory.

From above, she could see her father's mother holding Eva by her shoulders at the doorway of her father's bedroom. Her grandfather stood by, guarding any way of escape. Grandmother was forcing Eva to watch as Callie bent over her father's childhood bed, face down, as her father and uncle took turns abusing her.

Callie gagged, unable to make herself voice the words to her counselor or husband.

"What is it, Callie?" Greg asked anxiously.

Callie made motions and finally uttered a few words. It was enough for them to understand.

Finally when she could speak, she covered her face with her hands. "I can't ask Jesus to come here!"

"Callie, He already was. You just couldn't see Him."

Feelings of hatred began to bubble up in Callie's heart like hot lava. Her emotions swirled out of control.

"I hate them. I hate them. I wish they were dead. I wish I were dead. How could You let this happen?"

She stood face to face with her Lord.

Jesus knelt down in front of her, with tears in His eyes.

"Callie, I didn't want this to happen to you. This was not My will for you. Your father was a very hurt man who chose to go in the way of wickedness. But this anger is too big for you. Please Callie, let this anger go. Let Me hold it for you."

But Callie couldn't this time. She held onto the seething ball of pain.

"Callie, let me show you something," Jesus said gently.

Immediately the scene changed, and she saw her father as a boy, sitting on the curb outside his house, crying. She saw nasty, slimy imps clawing at his head.

Then she saw her father full of confusion, hurt, anger, and betrayal, at a place of decision. Would he give into the lies swirling around him, or would he resist?

She saw him give in.

"No, Dad, don't," she yelled, but the boy didn't hear her. Instead, she heard the voice of Jesus. "You see, Callie. Your father was once a child like you. He gave in to the demons trying to torture his mind. But you don't have to make the same choice. Let me have the hatred, daughter. In return, I will give you peace."

She chose well. Peace came.

৪৩৩

"Hey, Callie, it's Eva!" The next evening the nervous voice came through the phone line.

Eva? Why is she calling me. She never calls me. Callie's birth family was aware of her recovery journey, but only from a distance. All of them thought her foolish for "digging up bones" from the past.

"Hey, how's the counseling going?"

Weird. Weird that she would suddenly be interested in my counseling. Has she been talking to Mom?

"It's really tough right now, but it will get better. I know it will." Callie tried to keep her voice light, tried to make herself believe it.

"Well, sis, umm. I need to talk to you about something."

Oh no, here it comes.

But what came was different from what she expected.

"A few days ago, I began seeing these horrible images in my head. It was really freaking me out."

"Yeah?" Callie tried to keep her voice steady.

"Yeah." Eva cleared her throat. "It's gonna sound crazy, but it seemed important to tell you. It happened at Grandmother's house, you know, Dad's parents. The creepy house. And I was standing in the doorway of Dad's old bedroom, and Grandmother was holding my shoulders making me look in, and . . ."

As Eva continued to describe the scene, Callie felt a buzzing in her ears. *It was true. Eva remembers it too.*

"You've got to be kidding me," she finally choked out. "That's the same scene I saw in counseling last time."

"No way. That's so weird. Well, I told a friend about it, the one who knows about stuff like this, and she said there was some sort of a spiritual tie there with Dad's family. So we prayed for that to be severed, and I felt something happen, the tie being cut."

There was a pause, as if Eva had said all she needed to say.

"Thanks for letting me know," Callie said. "Umm, maybe we can talk about these things some more sometime?"

Eva laughed. "I don't think there's anything else! The tie was cut, and that's all there is. I just wanted to let you know about it."

Callie sighed. She could tell Eva was closing the door again. But at least she finally had something concrete to hold onto, some connection that what she was seeing in pieces and flashes was not just her overactive imagination. Maybe some of it was true.

ಬೂಡಿ

"I thought these images would stop." Callie gripped Greg's hand and gazed accusingly at Raymond. "I still see myself with that knife. I'm still scared for my children."

"We haven't gotten to everything yet," Raymond replied. "Sometimes healing is instantaneous. Sometimes it takes time and patience. Love is patient, young lady." He sounded the way she supposed a father ought to sound.

But thinking about the word "father" caused a nauseating sickness to crawl up Callie's abdomen. She squirmed in her seat. "No. This is too much!"

"What is too much? Who inside thinks this is too much? What do you think will happen if you see this?" Raymond gently prodded.

Had she spoken her feelings out loud or was Raymond now reading her thoughts?

"I'll lose my mind," she whispered.

"Callie, you didn't lose your mind when you went through this. In fact, your mind did a wonderful job of protecting you. You're safe now. Are you willing to look at this and receive healing for it?"

Again, the pages turned as the next chapter opened.

A dusty, winding dirt road twisted in front of the old station wagon. Strange tribal lanterns lined the path through the Everglades.

She, Daniel, and Eva sat cramped in the back seat, sweaty and arguing.

"Shut up back there," her father boomed. "You see those canals? There are alligators in there, and they'll jump out and eat anybody who misbehaves."

All the children became silent, except for Lita, the baby, who kept crying. In the passenger's seat, Mama tried to console her.

"Mama, where are we going?" Callie asked. "I thought we were going to the Kapok Tree."

But no reply came. Darkness enveloped them as her father parked the car. "Stay here until I come and get you," he ordered. Mama silently got out with the baby and followed him.

Through the smudged windows, Callie pressed her nose to see a ball of eerie, hazy firelight glowing in the distant. Heat waves hit the side of the vehicle, and she could see vague figures around the flames. *The dragon's breath.*

Callie's siblings all began to cry. She tried all she knew to do to comfort them, but nothing helped.

Her anxiety mounting, Callie gripped Greg's hand harder. "Helpless. I'm completely helpless. This is driving me crazy. Stop it. Stop crying. I'm suffocating."

"You can ask Jesus to come, Callie," Raymond said quietly.

"Jesus, are you here?"

Immediately, He flung open the car door and held her. "It's going to be OK, but there's more of this you need to see."

Dressed in a ghostly robe, her father returned to the family car. As he approached, he threw back his hood and opened the door.

"Come with me," he commanded. Mama stood silently behind him, a look of terror on her face.

Callie's confused mind thought she saw natives forced to march around the ring of fire. *Indians?*

Her father pressed a white substance onto her lips, and she choked it back. Everything blurred and spun.

Then there was blood, blood everywhere. On her, on the ground, on a table. Everything was covered in blood.

Some sort of priest stood over her. "Say this after me," he chanted. "I renounce Jesus as my Savior. My only savior is Satan. If I ever break this vow, my family and I will be. . . " The cursing went on and on.

Callie resisted. "I can't say that. No! I can't!" She struggled to somehow get away, but her father's hands firmly weighed on her shoulders.

"You must. Or I will kill you and your siblings." The cold words echoed over her, as a shroud of death already lay like a heavy black blanket across her soul.

What choice do I have? I am destined to burn in hell. She repeated the oaths as she was commanded. Her small frame shook with every vile word.

In the counseling room, Callie's head shook violently back and forth. "I can't be forgiven this. I can't be forgiven this," she muttered.

"What can't you be forgiven of?" Again, Raymond's voice pierced through her darkness.

"I was ordered to renounce Jesus Christ, and I did it. The man said he was my lord now." Callie heaved in the chair, holding her face in her hands, rocking back and forth like a child.

Greg gently rubbed her shoulder, while Raymond leaned in close to her face. "Sweet child, this was forced on you. This was not your choice. The only ones held accountable here are those who forced this on you. You did this drugged and against your free will. Any child in your place would have done the same thing."

Callie slumped forward. "Really?" She repeated the words. "Any child would've done the same thing?"

Finally she was able to ask the important question. "True Lord Jesus, what do you want me to know about this?"

Jesus stood in front of her with a golden light emitting from Him. "You belong to Me. You never belonged to them."

"But I feel like You could never forgive me for what I did there."

"Dear, dear child there is nothing for Me to even forgive. You have only done what you were forced to do. But just so that you can hear these words, I do forgive you. I love you so much."

Jesus offered His arms outstretched to Callie. At first she winced, imagining a fleeting image of Him hurting her like so many others had. But then she saw herself melt into His safe embrace.

He smiled. "Let's forgive them together," He said. And they did.

Finally Callie opened her eyes again. She was exhausted and perspiring. "Raymond," she asked, "how could God let me go through all this? Why didn't He stop it?"

"That's the question everyone wants to ask God. So, why don't you?"

She did. The answer came simply.

"Callie, I want to have children, not robots who are forced to love Me. Would I be any different from your abusers if I forced you to obey Me? People are made in My image, so they have the ability to choose good or evil.

"Daughter, I spoke truth to your father and mother, and to others as well, but they chose not to hear. Whether it was fear like your mother, or not wanting to see like her parents, or hatred like your father and his parents, they chose to believe those lies, instead of believing Me.

"The only way for Me to take you out was to take you to heaven or to destroy your family. That would have done more damage to how you viewed Me than the horrific things you endured. So I chose to give you the ability to dissociate, to tuck all the pain in little places inside, so that you wouldn't remember. I chose to hold you and love you through the suffering. I knew at the right time you would let Me in so we could heal all these wounds. That's what I'm doing now.

"Be at peace, dear one. Nothing can separate you from My love. Absolutely nothing."

That night for the first time in years, Callie slept peacefully. This time, she had begun to believe His words.

CHAPTER 12

Callie, age 9
Boykins, Virginia

The windows of the station wagon were rolled down, and the breeze blew Callie's long, bronze hair back from her face, cooling her hot cheeks. Cornfields rolled on like green sea waves, bordered by evergreen pine trees and sweet gum.

As they entered the small rural farming community that they would now call home, Callie wrinkled up her nose at a new odor wafting on the wind.

"What's the awful smell, Mama?" Eva exclaimed.

"Hogs, I think," said Mama, glancing at her father. Terrance's ears perked up as his nose poked the air, sniffing for the new tantalizing scents.

They pulled into the driveway of their new home, a parsonage sitting next to a small white church. While the others tumbled out of the car and began chasing each other in the driveway, Callie lingered by the car.

"It's really small for four children, Warren," Mama said quietly.

"The good Lord wants you to be thankful for what you have," Father snarled.

The next day a knock came at the door. Callie opened it to see a lanky girl about her age, tanned with bobbed brown hair, wearing ripped jean shorts and a thin t-shirt with a whiskey bottle printed on the front.

"Hey. My name's Diana. We'uns got the farm back there." She jabbed her finger toward the nearby cornfield rows. "I reckon you'uns are the new preacher's family. What's your name?"

A warmth filled Callie. Maybe she would have a friend, and maybe, for the first time, a best friend.

"Mama, can I go play?"

"Sure, Cal. Just stay outside out of my way."

Callie was good at that, staying out of the way. So, for the rest of the summer Diana and Callie were stuck together like peanut butter and jelly.

"Callie, my mama said you can stay for dinner tonight," Diana said one day. "But we got to fetch the chicken first for Grannie to kill." She pulled Callie by the arm to the chicken coop behind their house and began the chase, weaving in and around the frantic bird. Callie watched in amazement as she cornered the doomed victim.

With one swift motion, Grannie grabbed the bird by the neck and flipped her wrist. The next thing Callie knew, the decapitated chicken was dancing in the dirt, finally flopping to the ground.

"That's disgusting!" Callie exclaimed, covering her eyes.

"That there's life at my place." Diana chuckled.

After a dinner of fresh fried chicken, the two girls galloped out to see the stars and lie on the grass.

"You know if you ever go walkin' out in the woods, you gotta be real careful. Years ago the law came in here and blew up all the stills. They left big pits in the ground that are covered up now. If you'uns ever fall in one of those pits, no one will ever find ya."

"What's a still?" Callie asked.

"Moonshine still," Diana elaborated cryptically.

"You mean at night?"

"No. Not that kind of moonshine. Moonshine is a drink. Liquor."

Callie didn't say any more, but she stored these tips in the back of her mind.

Early the next morning, Diana appeared at the door. "Come on. Let's ride bikes," she urged. "We'uns got a extra one."

Hopping on the bikes, they rode past a white-washed brick building next to the country store. A sign above the door read, "Community Center." An odd symbol was displayed above the wording.

"What's that mean?" Callie asked. *It seems familiar, somehow.*

"Oh, that's just where the lodge meets." Diana said. "Let's go see Billy at the gas station."

They turned sharply to the left, skidding into the gravel lot next to the gas pump. Wiping his hands on a grease-stained rag in his belt, Diana's big brother sauntered out to greet them. "You girls need some gas?" He was teasing, but Callie thought she saw a strange glint in his eye.

Giggling, Diana shook her head. "I've just been giving Callie the grand tour."

৪৩

Camp Oukonunaka
est. 1957

The church bus filled with hot and sweaty children drove under the rustic log sign. Callie had loved driving through the mountains, but now her stomach churned from the ride.

When they finally arrived, the other girls ran outside to explore, but Callie cautiously inspected the girls' cabin, longing for a place she could retreat to if she needed escape. She observed the twenty bunk beds with granddaddy long-legs crawling on them and the dim buzzing light bulb swaying in the center.

But what stopped her cold was looking in at the girls' bathroom. Empty stalls with no doors for any privacy, and a lone, rusted shower head without even a curtain. *I'm not going to the bathroom in there.*

Her embarrassment heightened even more when the girls got dressed to go swimming and stripped right in the middle of their one-room cabin.

"Diana, I can't get dressed in here," Callie whispered fiercely.

Diana looked surprised. "All th' others are gettin' ready in here. It's OK."

But Callie's eyes begged for help. "I just can't."

Diana grabbed a towel and draped it around Callie. "You can dress behind this. Nobody'll see you."

Callie stripped off her clothes and pulled up her suit with great speed.

The days were filled with swimming and other activities. The evenings were filled with music, camp stories, and guilt-inducing sermons by her father.

One evening, an eleven-year-old boy grabbed Callie by the hand, urging her to walk with him in the moonlight. Callie resisted at first, but since she was almost twice as big as he was, she figured she could fight if she needed to. Hand in hand they strolled down a dark path where several other child lovers stood entangled in lustful embraces.

"Come on, Cal. Just one little kiss." He grabbed her by her waist.

"Pastor's coming! Hide!" The guilty parties scampered away like roaches, hopping over the cement walls around the pavilion, but Callie and her would-be lover stood frozen in fright.

"Callie is that you?" The flashlight blinded her. Ignoring the boy, her father grabbed her, digging his fingers into her arm, dragging her back, muttering. "I'll teach you not to embarrass me like this."

He might as well have stamped her with the scarlet letter for the rest of the week. Callie sobbed into her pillow that night, confiding in Diana her ultimate shame.

A true friend, Diana consoled her, falling asleep with their fingers entwined as their hands hung limp across the space between the beds.

৪১৫৪

The air grew brisker, the leaves began to show their colors, the hogs were fattened for the slaughter, and the new school year began. During the thirty-minute bus ride every day, sweaty, chatty children left Callie feeling trapped. Her stomach grew nauseated from the lurching and swerving. She ran down the aisle, only to vomit on the steps going out of the bus.

The putrid smell filled the bus, and the other children gagged. "Oh gross!" they shouted.

Callie kept her head down and covered her bright red face with her hands while Diana tried to comfort her.

The more time passed, the more tricks Callie tried to try to get Mama to let her stay home from school. When those didn't work, she begged for a note to stay in from recess, and Mama finally relented.

Day after day Callie laid her head down on her desk as the other children ran out to play. *I just don't fit in. I'm so different from the others. Something's wrong with me. I don't belong.*

"You, why do you always stay in?" The sharp tone of a classmate's voice made Callie raise her head. "You don't have anything wrong with you. Look at me." This girl motioned to the crutches and leg brace that were part of her daily routine. "I can't go run and play, but you can. You should be ashamed of yourself for staying in."

Callie's face grew scarlet from the sting of her condemning words. There was no peace, even in this almost empty classroom.

This girl's body was deformed on the outside, but Callie was deformed on the inside. How would this girl understand?

CHAPTER 13

Callie, age 11
Boykins, Virginia

October came, and with it came dread. Callie's father was making the final elaborate preparations for the haunted house their church would sponsor at the community center. All the kids at church were involved, and several adults.

"Cheryl, you'll dress up as a fortune teller. Here's your crystal ball. See, we'll project the image up through the ball like this." He shoved the glass globe in front of her. "Great effect!"

This was the only time of the year Callie's father was ever truly excited. Most of the time he was home he sat gazing at the television with a Bible on his lap, supposedly making his Sunday sermon notes. But now, he buzzed around like a wasp.

"I talked the mortician into letting us rent a real casket for the dracula to come out of. And the butcher at the grocer said I can have five pounds of sausage for the guts." On and on he went with his plans.

After all the preparations had been made, he announced, "Callie, you get to go through first. Our guinea pig." He rubbed his hands together.

"But Dad, I don't want to." She tried not to let her fear show. She knew fear was like bait to him.

But he wouldn't take no for an answer, so Callie had to climb through the entrance to the haunted house. She saw the guts lying beside a man they had pretended to cut up. Then Dracula jumped out, petrifying her.

But most of all, Callie was sickened to see her mama dressed like a gypsy hovering over the glowing crystal ball.

That night in bed Callie lay awake for hours, images from the haunted house playing repeatedly across the screen of her mind. Finally, she drifted off to sleep, but throughout the night she wrestled demons.

The clock struck three, startlingly her out of bed. Sweat soaked her nightgown. As she shook herself awake, she realized she had been dreaming about the dragon in the church next door again. His claws had almost gotten her this time.

There between the wall and the mattress she spotted her favorite book, *The Lion, the Witch, and the Wardrobe*. She'd read it only maybe 15 times, but she flipped to the first page, lovingly worn, and read, "Once there were four children . . ."[*]

Sleep and reading were Callie's only means of escape, but reading was the preferred choice. Through books she could travel where she chose to go, battling the foes in her stories, forgetting about the dragon.

For hours, she lay on her stomach, book in hands, legs crossed in the air behind her, until sleep finally won out.

---

[*] C.S. Lewis, *The Lion, the Witch, and the Wardrobe*. (New York, NY: Macmillan, 1950), p 1.

Finally she drifted off to her dream world of dwarves, fauns, talking beavers, a white stag, a lamp post, and Aslan.

ഇൗരു

Callie's eleven-year-old body had developed much more than others her age. As teenagers passed in and out of their home, one boy cornered her in the hallway and reached out his hand to grab her blossoming chest.

"What do think you're doing?" she shouted, knocking his hand away.

"Aww, come on." The boy grinned. "We all know pastors' daughters are easy."

From that day on, it seemed she was always fighting someone off.

One afternoon when only Callie and her father were home, to her surprise she looked up to see Diana's brother Billy sticking his head in her bedroom door. With a hunger in his eyes, he approached her, leaving no easy escape route.

Then he grabbed her, forcing her spread eagle onto the bed. His breath was hot and heavy on Callie's neck. "Come on, girl. Give me a real kiss." Determination and anger sparked in his eyes.

Callie struggled to get free. "Billy, I'll scream and my father will come rescue me!"

Billy face turned into a sneer. "Your father won't come," he mocked.

Callie went cold, knowing his words were true.

Outside the locked door, Terrance barked wildly. Suddenly, with no explanation, Billy released her wrists and walked out of the house to his car.

Trembling, Callie watched through the window as he drove away. Then she caught her breath and walked outside with Terrance, her faithful companion. She picked a muscadine grape and bit into the tough skin, expecting to find sweetness. But it was sour. Disgusted, she spit it out. Just like her family, it looked good on the outside, but the inside was sour and bitter.

&OCB

Later that summer, Diana skipped up the steps to Callie's back door and yelled through the screen. "Hey Cal! You wanna come to a sleepover with me and some other girls?"

"Sure, Mama won't care." *Mama never asks where I'm going.*

"Great. I'll be by to get you in a bit." Fifteen minutes later, Callie slung her sleeping bag in the back of a Ford pick-up truck driven by a teenage friend.

"Hey, let's go spinnin'," Diana yelled out the window as she swung her arm for her to get moving. Callie scrambled in the cab as they sped off. Turning onto a side dirt road, the driver shifted the gears, pressing down hard on the gas as the truck spun its wheels and kicked up a cloud. At the end of the road was a small clearing, where she quickly slammed on the brakes, sending the truck into a side spin.

"Yahoo. Let's try that again, but faster." The teenager hit the gas again, with Callie's head still spinning. She hung her head out the window so the breeze would ease her queasy stomach.

After spinning around until Callie felt like she was going to throw up, they finally pulled up to the house where the sleepover was happening. That night some boys showed up to play spin the bottle. It kept missing her, until the end. Embarrassed, she let the young boy kiss her on the lips. Then came "Truth or Dare." Callie preferred the dare, rather than being pressured to tell the truth, but decided to withdraw from the game faking a stomach ache, before her luck ran out.

Around midnight, she found herself in the ring of giggling girls. "If you don't want to get pregnant, you can have sex up until your period starts," one of the girls in the group declared.

Callie's chest tightened, her heart raced, and she began to sweat. She didn't know why this made her stomach twist. Though she was the youngest in the group, she had already begun her period.

℘☙

What's been the matter with Mama? She was more distracted and more irritable than Callie had ever seen her. Often, Callie would walk by her parents' bedroom and find her Mama crying into her pillow. Callie was left to take on the responsibility of both mom and dad to her siblings, a position they resented.

Offenses, once small, now ended with "Callie, go pick a switch from the front yard and come here." Her pale legs were often blistered with red welts.

Eventually Mama began sharing secrets with Callie, secrets she had been told never to tell. Turned out things had been done to Mama that never should have been done.

Mama was infected with a sickness of the soul.

"I've got to be strong for Mama," Callie whispered to Terrance as she nuzzled her face in his furry neck. She could barely even grasp what was happening to her family, but she knew she needed to be strong. She patted him on his shaggy head. "You're my best friend, aren't you, boy. You hear all my secrets." Terrence whined and laid his head on her lap.

That night a noise startled them all awake. Callie saw that Mama's eyes were wide with terror. "Someone's broken in!"

They opened the front door, and Callie saw her pup on the steps, dead.

"Oh God!" Callie cried. "Not my boy! My sweet boy! Why? Dear God, why?"

A single brick had been tossed through the window with a note. "You're next," was all it said.

The family decided to move again. This time it would be to Indiana.

Callie spent her last night with Diana. The two talked long into the night as they swore loyalty to one another. The next morning Callie woke early, tucked a tear-stained goodbye note under Diana's pillow, blew her a kiss goodbye, and tip-toed out of the room.

CHAPTER 14

Confession

(Fall 1991)

Alone, she stood like a chiseled statue surrounded by pitch black nothingness.

At first Callie couldn't even see her own hand in front of her, but after a minute her eyes began to adjust to the darkness smothering her. Slowly she placed one foot in front of the other, edging her way forward, stumbling over unseen obstacles in her path.

In the distance she saw what looked like a pinhole of light. All around her she could feel the slimy, cold presence of slithering things, reaching out to her from the sides of the tunnel. As the light began to grow, she could now see shadowy fingers grasping at her. Her pace accelerated.

"Can't stop here. Must keep going towards the light." She moved her lips, but no words came out. The dragon's breath smoldered near her spine, but she would not look back. Dodging left, then right, she avoided the touch of the clawing fingers.

The light grew brighter and brighter. She could now make out the end of the tunnel. Sprinting, she made her final push to throw herself forward into the brightness, and then, all at once, she burst into the glorious, dazzling light.

Blinded for a moment, she waited for her eyes to adjust to the brightness. She stood completely still as the scene came into focus all around her.

It was a field of vibrant greens, teals, browns, a deep blue sky, a rainbow of wild flowers, everything living. It was as if she was seeing for the first time, and she was overwhelmed with wonder.

As she looked back, she saw an ancient wooden door slam shut, gnarly fingers smashed in its jamb.

"What's wrong, Callie?" Greg's voice woke her fully, and she saw that she had jumped to her feet again, fist up, fighting her invisible foes. "Sweetheart, what are you doing?"

She pulled in a trembling breath. "It's that dream again. The one about the tunnel. I saw myself break through this time. I wasn't sucked in." A spark of hope lit in her voice as she crawled back in to bed and pulled the sheets up tight around her neck.

"Sweetie, I feel like you're always somewhere else." Greg touched her arm.

"But I'm not withholding from you." *Grandma always said you have to keep your man satisfied or he'll go else-where.* Callie did her duty, mechanically giving what Greg wanted.

But who wants mechanical lovemaking? Feeling Greg pull away, she knew he longed for closeness not just of her body, but of her heart.

The next time in Raymond's office, Greg expressed his exasperation. "I just want her to want to, you know, to not be just *there*."

Feeling exposed, Callie felt her leg begin to shake violently. Greg gently placed his hand on her knee to soothe her, but she jerked away. "Don't touch me," she said sharply.

Raymond glanced at Greg as if to signal, "Back off. Let me handle this."

Greg's face grew red with embarrassment.

As Callie automatically closed her eyes, she saw a dark figure standing at the door of her bedroom. Her ten-year-old self lay completely motionless as if that would make her invisible, trying to give no indication she saw or heard the man approaching her. "I can't see who it is," she said.

"Ask Jesus, Callie," Raymond said gently.

"Jesus, who is this?" All at once she saw the twisted look on her father's face as he approached her. It was no use to resist as his heavy body lay on her small form. Through the shame he craftily worked, she was convinced that she was of no consequence. Curled in a fetal position, she wept as her father exited the room, having stripped her of all dignity, all childhood.

He said he loves me. This is what love is like. He said that I wanted this, to be treated this way. Does love strip naked like this? Does it leave this hole in my gut? He also said it was all my fault. That he couldn't help himself. He told me never to tell anyone. Especially Mama. Is Mama not enough for him?

The thoughts tumbled through her mind, a confusing mixture of adult with child.

What if Mama saw me like this? She got sick to her stomach. Thoughts swirled through her head like a tornado. Shame, guilt, hatred, and condemnation soiled her heart. *How could I tell Mama anyway? Mama would hate me.*

As all this played on the screen of her mind, Callie had been reacting in her chair in Raymond's office, the look on her face revealing her shame and grief.

Greg shifted in his chair as anger lit his face.

"Callie, where is Jesus?" Raymond said the words again.

"I can't invite Him here. I just can't. He's so good. And I'm so . . ." her words trailed off.

"Callie, nothing your father did to you made you anything less than God's daughter. You didn't deserve to be treated that way."

"But I craved his love," Callie shot back. "I let him do this."

"Callie, you didn't want your father to sneak into your bedroom and do those things to you. Your father manipulated you to get what he wanted. I know this is hard to understand, but listen to me. Good fathers don't rape their daughters. God doesn't rape His girls. Normal fathers would never even see their daughter that way. It would make them sick."

This was revelation truth for her. She turned towards Greg. "Do you mean, Greg, you never look at our girls that way?"

"Oh, dear. No. Never have I thought about that with our girls. And thinking about how the man you call father has done this to you, it makes me want to kill him."

"Callie," said Raymond, "your father must have had something just as bad or worse happen to him. He's doing what was done to him."

"But you're making excuses for him," Callie protested. "What he did was wrong. I hate him. I wish he were dead." The outburst surprised her.

"I'm not making excuses for his sin. He'll answer to God for what he's done. But it may help you to forgive him, if you understand this. What does Jesus say about this?"

Gently, she heard the voice within her heart say, "Let Me be his judge, Callie. Only I can be."

As she spoke the words of forgiveness, she saw herself being picked up off the bed and placed on her feet beside Jesus on the floor. The Prince of Peace took off her torn, blood-stained nightgown. From behind him, he took a clean, delicately-stitched gown, brilliantly white. "For me?" Callie hung her head. "How can that be?"

"Because in my sight you are pure, My daughter. You are a pure virgin." He pulled a white muslin curtain between her and the bed.

ROCR

Over the next several months in Raymond's office Callie re-lived one heart-breaking assault after another, each a different piece holding the same lies and shame. Teenage boys throwing her down in the woods at camp, trapped in a truck on a dirt road, more scenes with her father and others, the memories came bubbling up as if to say, "Me next. Help me here."

In each place Jesus always met her, always removing the shame and the lies, helping her to forgive, always reinstating her as pure and lovable. Each time Callie tried to believe it a little more, but it was so hard.

One night, after Callie had finished reading to the girls, she tiptoed to her own bedroom and was surprised to see Greg sitting there on the bed, wringing his hands.

What's wrong? She sucked in her breath. *Did someone die? Maybe he lost his job. Or he's worried about the checkbook.*

On guard, she plopped down next to him and hugged her pillow.

"Callie," Greg stuttered, "there's something that I've felt so guilty about," he stared vacantly at his white knuckles. "If I don't tell you now, I might explode."

Callie scooted closer to the edge of the bed near the door.

"You know when you asked me when we were engaged if I was a virgin, and I said yes?" *Was that relief she heard in his voice?*

Callie nodded her head slowly, and her face went numb. *Oh no, God, what's he getting ready to say?* She had always been completely honest with Greg, at least as much as she could. She had thought that trust was the foundation of their marriage.

The words tumbled out of Greg's mouth about the girls he had slept with in college. How he'd meant to tell her time and time again, but didn't want to hurt her. How he had lied to get her to marry him. "It was because I loved you, and I didn't want to lose you."

He kept going, dropping bombshell after bombshell. "And Cal, I struggled with porn a lot as teenager. There were times when were first married, when you couldn't have sex, that I looked at porn instead."

This last was the greatest blow. "I've prayed about this time and time again. I've just so felt the conviction of the

Holy Spirit. I had to confess this to you." And now Greg seemed to think that the pressure was all off his shoulders.

But he had dumped it on Callie's.

I'm not enough. I'll never be enough.

A vile laugh echoed through her mind.

The only man she had ever mostly trusted had violated her too. *What else has he not told me?* She looked at Greg as the enemy now.

"Hon, I'm really sorry. Will you forgive me?" Greg's sincerity caught her off guard. Couldn't he see that he had created a new wound, somehow even greater than the others she had been bearing?

"I can't." She burst into tears, the heels of her hands pressed into her eyes. "Why now, Greg?" She couldn't trust him. How could she trust him ever again?

In the days that followed, Callie began regularly checking Greg's pockets for slips of papers for women's names or phone numbers. If he went out, he had to call her to tell her where he was and exactly when he would be home.

"You need to reconcile this, Greg," Raymond advised when they next met. "You don't understand what you did to violate Callie's trust. I know it brought you relief to confess, and the truth needed to come out, but you devastated her. Remember the marriage class I taught on rebuilding trust. Let her ask you the questions, and be willing to answer them honestly. You have to rebuild the trust you've lost."

That was not an easy task.

With Greg's confession and with the memories of her own abuse heavy on her heart, Callie felt as if she had lost trust in all men, especially men in leadership. Desperate for a friend, she sought out Edith's counsel once more.

Callie could no longer hold back the question that burned on her lips. "Edith, you were married to your husband for more than thirty years before he passed." She took a deep breath. "Was he faithful to you all those years?"

With a tense shifting in her chair, Edith tersely answered, "Well, of course he was."

Callie rushed on about Greg's confession and her inability to trust any man, but abruptly, Edith raised her hand for Callie to stop.

"I can't go on meeting like this, Callie. I have to get back to the store." With that, Edith pulled a thick curtain between them, slamming shut their friendship.

Shocked, Callie walked out the door.

Not another word was spoken between them as friends.

ಬಿಉಣ

"We should do something fun together and go on a vacation," Greg restlessly argued with Callie. "We need something happy in our lives. A good distraction."

He's tired of doing penance. Callie grimaced. "I don't think I can travel right now, Greg. I just feel so unstable. I mean, do I look like someone who's stable?" She pointed to the notes she had tagged all over the medicine cabinets. "God loves me! I am valuable. I am His."

"You know why I put them there?" Callie asked. "Because every time I open the cabinet doors, all I see is myself overdosing and ending this pain." *I feel guilty about killing a fly, why in the world would I want to kill anyone, including my-*

self? Nothing makes sense. "I'm so tired of fighting, Greg. I just want rest. Not travel."

"But a change of pace might help the whole family out of this glum."

"Greg, please. I don't think I can."

"Callie, come on and try."

"But remember our last time at the beach?"

The mantra had been "have fun," so she had given it her best effort to forget the pain, settle her mind, and enjoy it through her children's delight. But instead she had found herself arranging her sleeping children between her and the sliding glass door to the balcony, because she felt something trying to pull her out the door and over the railing.

The thought of ever going there again—or any place like it—caused her chest to tighten.

But Greg's relentless pleading finally made her give in.

The morning they were to leave, the children were already in the van, when the phone rang. Greg answered it, and Callie saw the color drain from his face.

Tears welled in Greg's eyes. "Pastor Matt passed away this morning. The cancer had weakened his body. He fell and didn't get up again."

So much for a happy vacation.

A week later, they sat once again with Pastor Matt's best friend, Raymond. "Why did he have to die?" Callie's words rang with anger, her fists clenched. "Why did God take him?"

Raymond simply sat there and wept with her and Greg. No answer seemed sufficient.

Grief had become her constant companion. It seemed to be more than Callie could bear.

As time passed and Callie couldn't crawl out of the hole of grief, Raymond expressed his concern. "Callie, I understand you're experiencing grief, but this is too much. I'm very sad too. Pastor Matt was one of my closest friends. But I'm not sinking into a hole of depression like you are. Are you willing to look back to see where all this grief is coming from?"

"Yes, because it hurts. It hurts so badly that it's hard to breathe. Am I gonna die?" She closed her eyes, leaning back into the sofa.

The memories came fast and hard.

At first, she saw herself as a young child, walking through the lonely hallways of her great-grandmother's house in the middle of the night. The heavy back door was ajar. She tiptoed out in her nightgown to the sounds of men's angry voices in the yard. The breeze blew her gown around her ankles. She opened the door more and peeked out, gazing over the wooden railing of the wrap-around porch. In the distance she saw the backsides of hooded shadows looking towards a burning cross. It felt cloudy, like a dream.

Then it shifted.

She was inside the church next to the parsonage, clutching tightly to her mama and siblings. The stained-glass windows were dark.

The small sanctuary where her father recited his weekly Biblical brow beatings was now filled with confusion and desecration. The dragon was in full force, blazing its fiery breath of death, flipping its tail, destroying everything in its path.

Callie watched as dark creatures, tied up, were death-marched down the center aisle, to be an offering to a different god. The baptistry became the entrance to eternity for the poor souls marked for death. A fire blazed behind the church to dispose of the evidence, and a deep hole was dug to hide the charred remains.

Sick. On the couch in Raymond's office, Callie lurched and gagged and wretched. Greg put his hand on her back while Raymond held a trash can in front of her.

The scene changed again.

A stream came into view, weaving through a wooded area. The ground was covered in sand, and a tree branch hung low with a rope flung over its bough. Callie vaguely recognized the park her family had frequented in the summers.

Figures of men stood surrounding the tree. Angry, excited voices shouted curses, as a hunched-over being was brought forth, his head covered with a bag. A noose had already been placed around his neck as they led him like cattle, prodding him along.

Callie covered her eyes as the lynching was completed.

"Why, why did they do these horrible things?" Her heart beat wildly at what had just been uncovered, and she felt overwhelmed with grief for the victims of the crimes. She thought she would faint.

"Often a whole community would be involved in these crimes," Raymond said. "I know it's very hard to look at and understand, but remember they tried to make you forget all these things for a reason, so no evidence would be left."

"But I felt like it was my fault. Like I committed the crimes." She wept bitterly, her tears falling to her knees. How could she explain the heavy weight she carried?

"Why do you feel like it was your fault, Callie?" Greg spoke this time.

"Because it was my family who was involved in this, who maybe even was the cause of this. Don't you remember what that man said in the counseling group? When he heard some of my story, he said if it had been in Old Testament days, our whole family would have been stoned to death. He was right. We all deserved to die." She felt the complete responsibility of their sin on her shoulders, crushing her beneath its weight.

"And don't you also remember what Kimee prayed over you that day?" Greg interjected. "She prayed a prayer of forgiveness and release over you for what they had done." Kimee was a beautiful Kenyan doctor who had also been in the class that day.

Callie stared ahead, not answering.

"Callie?" It was Raymond's voice. "Even though everything you participated in was forced on you, you're holding this against yourself. Jesus doesn't hold this against you."

"Jesus," Callie prayed, "what do you want me to know about this?"

"Daughter, I don't hold you accountable for the sins of your father or his family, but I know you need to hear these words from Me. Sweetheart, though you didn't do anything wrong here, you are forgiven. Your hands are clean. You can stop torturing yourself. You can't make yourself suffer enough to pay for these sins, but I already have paid for them."

"Yes, Lord. I receive Your love, and I release myself from needing to try to pay for these offenses. And I trust You to set things right with my family for committing these crimes."

She meant every word, but sometimes you must release over and over before release is complete.

Layer upon layer, peeling back over and over.

She was so weary of it all. All she wanted to do was go home and sleep forever.

Part 3

"You surround me with songs and shouts of deliverance."

Psalm 32:7 (Amplified)

CHAPTER 15

Tipping Point
(Fall 1992)

Holding up the pink-lined test, Callie slowly lowered herself on the side of the bed, stunned. "Greg. Honey. Come here." She wagged the stick so he could see it. "I think I'm pregnant."

"Callie, that's great." Greg's eyes gleamed at the thought of perhaps finally having a son. Since they had been married, he had longed to have a boy as their own.

If it had been another time, another season, she would have been elated too.

"You don't understand." Callie pulled her knees up to her chest. "I can't have a baby. Not now. I'm taking that anxiety medicine the doctor put me on. I can't live without that."

Greg's confused, hurt glance made her heart sink, and she burst into tears. "Oh, how can I handle this? I can't do this. Greg, you don't understand."

Callie's body had simply become unable to handle the task of digging through the wreckage of her past. The medicine had taken the edge off of those mental processes, bringing some relief. But thinking of having to face herself unaided caused sheer panic.

A few days later they listened to the family doctor confirm what they already knew. "Yes, you're pregnant," he stated matter of factly. "We're going to have to wean you off that anxiety medicine."

Callie's face went pale.

"Well, you don't want an abortion, do you?" The doctor looked back and forth from Callie to Greg.

"No, doctor. We're thrilled to be having another baby." Greg couldn't hide his excitement.

"Oh, good. I'll be right back with a plan for you to get off that medicine safely."

I don't want to do anything to hurt the baby, but I don't think I can live without the medicine. I think I'm addicted to it. Callie's thoughts filled with images of losing control and destroying her family. *Oh, what will I do?*

She was still moaning inside when the doctor returned with the instructions.

Why doesn't the pain just end? Thoughts of taking her own life tempted her again, but she knew she couldn't do that to her young girls.

All the way home, Callie's thoughts raced. Little Beth had already taken on more responsibilities for her younger sisters than any seven-year-old should have to do, and with a new baby, that would only increase. *I've done to my daughter what was done to me. Why can't I be stronger?*

Why doesn't the pain end? Her mind went in crazy directions. *I should kill myself. No, I can't do that to my children. I should run away. That will be better for them. Or maybe I should just disappear. They would be so much better off without me.*

As Greg drove in stoic silence, Callie hid her face in her hands. *Why didn't you give them a whole mama? I'm just a broken mess.*

The voice that spoke to her heart was a familiar one.

I gave them the best mama for them. You.

But that felt impossible to believe.

༄༅

Just two days later Callie called the baby doctor to see if she could stay on the anxiety medication, but what she heard shocked her.

"That's a category 4 drug. You have to come off that right now."

"Cold turkey?"

"Yes, absolutely right now. No weaning. Don't take it again. It could cause permanent damage to your baby."

"But, my family doctor said it would take a month to come off."

"No. Now." And the phone hung up.

"Permanent damage," she repeated to herself. If she continued taking the drug now, it would be like aborting her baby. The thought made her feel like vomiting.

"Greg, you have to get rid of this medicine, so I won't be tempted to take it." She explained her last conversation with her OBGYN. Greg gladly flushed the white tablets down the toilet.

Over the course of the next 24 hours, violent shaking, extreme anxiety, and insomnia hit Callie's weak body like a wrecking ball. Greg held her and spoke truth to her, but day after day she was afraid she would die.

What have I done?

"I haven't slept in a week." Callie spoke weakly into the phone. "There's got to be something you can give me."

"We can't. You'll have to wait for your first appointment, or you can go to the emergency room."

But if I go to the ER, they'll put me back on the medicine I'm trying to get off, and they'll also see I'm losing it, and I'll end up in a mental hospital. What will happen to my girls? She didn't reply to the nurse, but her mind raced with images of being put in a straitjacket trapped in a padded white room.

I remember you were always afraid of going insane, Mama. It didn't happen to you, but now it's happening to your daughter.

As the days passed, Callie could barely walk to the bathroom unassisted. The girls climbed in bed with her, asking her to read a story, but the words all blurred together and she couldn't even hold the book.

"It will be OK, Mommy!" said Beth, snuggling up next to her. "Can I pray for you?"

"Yes, Beth, please pray."

Seven-year-old Beth's voice quaked with emotion. "God, Mommy's really sick. Please heal her and help the baby too. In Jesus' name. Amen." Gently she touched her mother's face. "Do you feel better now?"

"Better, Bethie. Thank you for praying for me. God is healing me. Don't worry, baby." Callie brushed off the tiny tears that had wet Beth's soft cheeks.

∞∞∞

Before long Mary came, a new friend who had only recently entered Callie's life, an answer to prayer. Bubbling with joy and always bearing a large grin on her face, Mary came to clean

Callie's house and feed her hungry family, somehow able to do all that in addition to caring for her own six children.

"You're such a great mom," Callie said weakly. *You're a much better mom than I am. That's what I really mean.* Tears filled her eyes. "If only . . ."

Mary placed her hand on Callie's arm, rubbing it gently. "Beautiful, you are a great mom. You just need a little help right now."

"But why does God allow such bad things to happen to His kids? Why does He let us go through so much pain? Wasn't Jesus supposed to have borne our pain?" The questions hung in the air.

Mary looked directly into Callie's clouded eyes. "I don't know, Callie. But I know He is good. He is a good, loving Father."

Callie had no grid for a good father, a father who loved her, but she saw joy dancing in the deep blue eyes of her friend, a joy she had never felt.

I'm so, so tired. So tired of living. So tired of trying. So tired of trying to do what's right. So tired of trying to find answers to the pain. So tired of trying to find the one memory that will finally be the last. So, so tired.

That night as she lay next to Greg, Callie's breathing became shallow. In and out. It was all she had strength left to focus on. Each living breath. *Jesus. Am I dying?*

No answer came, but peace finally did. The anxiety slipped away and a blanket of peace enveloped her. *Am I going to wake up in heaven?* She embraced her belly, rubbing it softly. *Little one, this has nothing to do with you. Mommy loves you. Don't give up, little one.*

"Jesus, I'd lay down my life for this baby," she cried softly, wetting the side of her pillow.

That's because you're a good mother. You would never do anything to hurt your children. You'd lay down your life for them.

She closed her eyes and finally drifted off into a semi-sleep state, somewhere between dreams and reality.

ЮCЗ

"You said I could see the doctor," Callie blurted out. "When do I get to see the doctor?"

"Oh, this is your first visit," the nurse replied blandly. "You won't see a doctor for three more weeks."

Curse words flew through Callie's mind. Here she was almost too weak to sit up, leaning on the office desk with Greg supporting her, and this nurse was going over the new-mommy paperwork as if this were her first child and as if she were not in desperate condition.

"But you don't understand. I haven't slept in weeks. My anxiety is through the roof."

The nurse looked at her coldly. "Well, your hormones go into a different state when you're pregnant. Same with menopause. You better get used to it."

Callie almost kicked a hole in the desk. *How dare she.* She began rocking back and forth to control the volcano inside, her face red with rage. "I have to see a doctor today." She tried to control her voice, but her teeth were gritted. "The nurse on the phone promised me."

The nurse raised her eyebrows and stood up. "Hold on just a minute."

Finally the doctor came in. "There's nothing we can give you, but I can admit you to the hospital. I think that would be the best thing."

"Won't they put me back on the medicine you told me I had to come off of?"

"Yes. And they'll give you a thorough checkup."

"The answer is no. I've already made up my mind. I must be almost through the withdrawal, and I will not go through this again."

"Then go home, take a nice hot shower, and try to relax."

But when they got home, there was a message on the machine. "Mrs. McCormick, you need to go back on the anxiety medication tonight or else check into the hospital. We've learned from the pharmacist that going off that medication suddenly can be life-threatening."

Callie's heart raced as Greg refilled the prescription. *No no no no no.*

"You have to take this pill, Callie," Greg urged. "Your life depends on it."

No no no no no, Callie thought as she swallowed the pill.

The next day she began to show signs of miscarriage.

I wasn't strong enough. The accuser's finger wagged in her face, as he jeered at her, taunting. *I've killed my baby.* The guilt was almost too much to bear.

But in spite of the accusations, she heard hopeful words in her mind, some familiar, some new.

You have come to the end of yourself, and you have not lost your mind, nor have you hurt your children. You would give your life for your children. When you think of this child, you will see this time as a turning point.

A friend from a Bible study, a tall, noble, ebony-skinned woman, came to visit that afternoon. She leaned over Callie, kissing her forehead.

"Callie, I knew you were going to lose this baby. But God wants you to see that this time in your life is a turning point."

Callie was stunned. How could this woman know what she had already heard?

Greg was silent with grief. The girls couldn't understand why the baby had gone to heaven. Neither could Callie. All she could do was place the child in the hands of Jesus and trust.

It was one of the hardest things she had ever done.

CHAPTER 16

Callie, age 12

Madison, Indiana

The forested plain turned into rolling hills, rolling hills turned into smoky blue mountains, smoky blue mountains turned into more rolling hills, which finally turned into the Ohio River Valley.

A large steel bridge over troubled waters was the last thing separating the great Kentucky blue from her new home. Callie's father had taken a job at a local community college as the campus pastor.

They pulled up to a rundown house, tall and skinny, smashed up next to the ones on either side, with only narrow alleys between. It was a far cry from the isolated country home.

Callie's stomach grew queasy at the thought of middle school approaching. *Will I make any friends?* This big city jungle was so different from the back country of Virginia.

This school had a choir, and Callie did love to sing. That fall she took the stage with thirty other middle schoolers.

There she squinted into the blinding lights in search of her family. There were Mama and her siblings . . . but no Father, as usual.

Callie loved hearing all the voices flowing in harmony. "Whose woods these are I think I know. His house is in the village though. He will not see me stopping here to watch his woods fill up with snow."[*]

Don't buckle your knees. Don't buckle your knees. Their teacher had warned about students passing out. That was all Callie could think about.

"The woods are lovely, dark, and deep. But I have promises to keep. And miles to go before I sleep."

Her voice quavered, her palms grew sweaty and cold, and her heart palpitated. She felt lightheaded, her stomach queasy, but she refused to buckle her knees.

Soon the concert was over, and Mama hugged her. Callie breathed in deeply. *I did it.*

☜☞

But before long Mama announced that they'd be moving again—which meant Callie would be changing schools . . . again. *At least we're moving into a two-story house where I can have my own room.* Callie tried to console herself.

At the new school, Callie hated the embarrassment and humiliation of "shower day," when the gym teachers required all

---

* Robert Frost, "Stopping by Woods on a Snowy Evening" from *The Poetry of Robert Frost,* edited by Edward Connery Lathem. Holt, Rinehart, and Winston, 1967.

the girls to strip and shower naked. She saw that the other girls hated it too.

But her new friend Rey and her other classmates had a strange admiration for Callie as the only kid in their class with a father. One day when they got off the bus stop, Rey asked, "Callie, what's it like to have a dad?"

"What do you mean?" Callie shifted her weight back and forth, trying to act casual, but she didn't know how to answer.

"I mean, you're the only kid in school with a dad. My dad ditched my mom and me when I was a baby. Mom works all the time. What's it like?"

"Well, I don't see him much. I mean, he's not around much. When he's there, he says he loves me, but . . ." Her voice trailed off.

Then suddenly with great enthusiasm she asked, "Hey did you see the guy at school yesterday? He looks like a member of the Sugarhill Gang. He sings like them too." Then she added, "He's performing at the park on Saturday. You wanna go? He's kind of cute."

"Sure. That's sounds cool. Let's do it."

The diversion worked. For the moment, she was off the hook. She never wanted to have to talk about her father.

༄༅

"You're going to have a new brother," Callie's mom declared wearily one afternoon.

"Are you pregnant, Mom?" Eva asked.

"Ha. No. That would not be possible. Your father took care of that. No, your father wants to foster a young teen."

That evening Callie's father brought home a skinny, shy young man who wore jeans a bit too short for his long legs.

He pushed his dirty blonde hair out of his eyes, took his seat at the opposite end of the table, and shoved spaghetti in his mouth.

"Tell them your name." Her father glared at the teenager.

"Dean," he mumbled. But glancing up at Callie's look of pity, he smirked.

After cleaning up, Callie and Dean walked into the small patch of grass in the backyard. "Come on, Callie," Dean jeered. "Let me see what you've got." He planted his feet solidly on the ground between the house and shed. "Throw a punch at me. You can't hurt me."

So Callie threw back her arm and landed a blow through his upheld fists, directly on his nose.

"Ouch!" Blood spurted from his nostrils. Shocked, he shouted, "Good one!" She watched his eyes widen with respect. She wouldn't have to worry about this one.

But as time passed, Dean closed up more and more. He taught Daniel how to roll and smoke grass, but other than that he barely spoke to anyone in the family. What was wrong with him? What made him so wary, so distrusting?

One night she found out, when Dean walked right into her bedroom without knocking. Callie spun around to face him.

He gazed into her eyes, nose to nose with her.

"You know what your father is?"

Callie shook her head vigorously, willing him to silence, wishing she could plug her ears.

But he didn't take the hint. "Your father is a pervert. And he prefers boys."

He might as well had punched her in the nose, as the blood drained away from her face.

Callie shrank back with a look of acknowledgement and horror. To hear such words said so matter-of-factly, so bluntly, sent all her defense mechanisms into panic mode. "Just leave, Dean. Get out of here."

"Oh, I'm getting out of here all right, and I'm going to expose that bastard you call 'father' for what he really is."

He was true to his word. The following day, he was gone.

ଌଓଌ

"I hate him!" Mama screamed.

Shocked, Callie flipped around from doing the dishes to face her mom. A coffee mug flew by her head.

It barely missed her, crashing into the wall and shattering all over the floor.

"Mom, what's wrong? What are you doing?"

Mama sunk her face in her hands, sobbing. "I can't do this."

"But Mom, you and Dad were going for counseling. Didn't it help?"

"That was useless. He blamed everyone else for his problems," Mama seethed. "The only thing he said was that your grandfather is the pervert who screwed me up. He won't come clean of anything."

"But what will we do?" Callie tried to keep her voice calm, but she was shaking.

With a wild look of desperation, Mama said, "Callie, Dean threatened to report your father. This may be my chance to get out of this hell."

"Would you leave us?"

But Mama didn't answer.

Callie went numb. *She really might do this. She really might abandon us.*

But as it turned out, it wasn't Mama who left.

Just a few nights later, Mama yelled at her husband, "He's going to report you! He promised! What are we going to do?"

A strange look flashed across her father's face. Was it contempt? Fear? Callie didn't know. What she did know was that the next day he packed his bags and was gone.

That night, Callie gazed at the sky out her bedroom window. *Now there won't be anyone in my class at school with a dad.*

She sighed.

Why couldn't I have held my family together? What did I do wrong?

The smell of the window screen rust blended with the smell of Callie's salty tears as a light breeze blew through the window.

What's going to happen to us? I'm all alone. God, do You hate us? Where are You?

Mama spiraled down into a dark hole. "I can't go home to your grandfather," she explained. "Separation is like adultery in our church. He'll crucify me if I go home, especially being a pastor's wife. We'll just have to try to make it here."

Mama finally found a job as a check-out clerk at a grocery store.

Three weeks later, she tossed a legal document on Callie's bed. "Your dad filed for divorce," she said sullenly. "And in his letter, he's trying to get out of paying child support. Says that it's all my fault. I'm the reason our marriage failed."

For days Mama wouldn't get out of bed.

"Mom, you've got to go to work," Callie urged. "They're calling and asking about you. And a man showed up at the door this morning saying he was going to evict us."

The word *evict* sparked a determination in Mama. She climbed out of bed and got herself to work. But within a week, they were packing boxes and moving again, to a hole in the wall she could afford.

But Mama had made a mistake. She had thought she could store all their precious belongings in the shed behind the rental house until they could come back to get them. But when they returned a few days later, they found the shed padlocked with all their toys, treasures, and memories trapped behind the metal siding and broken glass window.

"There's nothing we can do. We're too late," Mama said. "I'm so sorry kids."

Through the broken glass, Callie could make out the soft grey head of her sock monkey dangling out of a box. *Oh, my precious monkey. I'll never see him again.* She pressed her nose against the broken glass window as tears streamed down her hot cheeks.

CHAPTER 17

A Rescue Line

(Winter 1993)

Callie could now get out of bed, but dizziness meant that walking in a straight line remained difficult for months. The basic freedom of driving, which she had always viewed as a means of escape, was suddenly taken away.

Doctor visit after doctor visit did little to offer results or help. "The only way this kind of thing can happen is through extreme trauma, like a stroke," one doctor had told her. His words were less than comforting.

One sleepless night after another left her so weary. *I just want to sleep, Lord. Sleep forever.* Then some old words floated into her consciousness. *But I have miles to go before I sleep.*

Will I ever be able to function well again? Will I even survive? Day after day the depression demons plagued her.

"I've got to go to California for a week of training," Greg announced one evening.

"What? When? I can't function without you." *I'll lose my mind while Greg's gone. What's wrong with me? I'm just like my father, that's it. I'm going to destroy my family. I'm going to hurt my children.* "Please, Greg, can't you figure out something else?"

"I'll lose my job if I don't go." Greg dashed that hope with a word. "But I'll ask my mom to check in on you and the girls."

Ugh. I never measure up to what she thinks I should be. "Can your mom help the kids with their baths?" *Nope, not going to tell him that I keep seeing the children drowning in the bathtub.*

"Sure. It will all be OK, sweetheart. I promise." He kissed her on the forehead. "And besides, you're stronger than you think."

You don't understand at all. I'm not strong. You need to see me the way I am now, not the artificial way I was when you married me.

"I wish I could ask Edith for help." *She was too busy to come when I was on my deathbed. Why would she come now? Oh, I wish we could go to a different church.*

It was as if Greg read her mind. "You know we're both hearing that the Lord wants us to stay at this church, even if things are . . . different . . . with Edith."

Callie winced. She couldn't think about that now. "Mary? Can Mary help?"

"Oh yes, I forgot to mention that. Mary said any time you need anything, give her a call."

Somehow Callie knew. *With Mary, I won't have to act put together. It won't matter if I'm a wreck. She'll accept me just the way I am.*

While Greg was gone, Mary came over.

"Callie, I see you in quicksand." Mary sat on the other end of the sofa, just the way Callie had seen her in her dream the previous night. "The harder you try to escape, the more you sink. I see Jesus standing on the side, throwing you a rope. He's asking you to grab onto it, and He will pull you out."

"Yes, Lord, I'm grabbing on." Callie murmured the prayer.

And somehow, over the next several months, He did.

One morning while lying in bed, Callie stared at her easel that she hadn't used since her first child was born.

Callie, I want you to start painting again. The whisper seemed to linger.

"I can't even see straight, Lord. How can I paint? What do I paint?"

I want you to begin painting your story.

That afternoon she stood squinting at a blank canvas. She tried to focus her eyes on the end of the paint brush,

But everything went blurry. *You'll have to help me, Jesus.*

Brush stroke after stroke, she began painting her pain, fears, healing, and triumph.

There on the canvas emerged a young girl wearing a red dress, nestled next to her Savior.

೮Ის

After Greg returned home, Callie was eager for their next session with Raymond.

"I don't understand why I still have all these thoughts of hurting my kids," she began. "Surely by now I've dealt with everything."

"You've been through so much, Callie. But you are not your father. You're facing these things because you love your kids and your husband and want to be free. Do you see that the fact that you're concerned for your children's safety means you're a good mom, not a bad one?"

Callie's body began shaking.

"Since you're still fighting yourself, that means someone inside still believes the lie that you're like your father."

"But my own mom said that was true." Callie began to sob.

"Callie, your mom spoke out of her own fears. It's time to see what's holding that lie in place."

Callie nodded. At home with her children, she had to keep these memories at bay, had to keep pressing them back behind the closet door. But here, she didn't need to protect her little ones from herself. Here, she could let the memories come.

Her mind drifted back to the rundown shotgun house in Indiana. She winced.

"I'm in bed with my father in my parents' bedroom." She covered her face. "He's . . . he's . . . " She couldn't say the words.

A sudden look of horror spread across Callie's face. "I see my mom open the door. She saw what was happening. Her face turned gray and she shut the door. She knows. She knows, and she ignored me."

Callie doubled over as if she had been punched in the stomach. The keening wail coming from her sounded like a wounded animal.

He's making me like him. I wish I'd never been born. Then she spoke the words she was hearing in her mind. "I am nothing. Only here to be used."

The condemnation poisoned like viper venom.

"Callie, that is not who you are. Not how God sees you." She could hear Raymond's firm voice echoing in the room.

"Jesus, help me."

Immediately she saw Him right there in her parents' room with her, standing beside the bed.

"This is not who you were made to be. You are My daughter, and I paid the highest price for you. This is not how you deserve to be treated."

"But why did Mom abandon me?" Callie sobbed. "She walked in. She saw it, and she walked back out!" She could hardly catch her breath.

"Honey, your mom didn't know what to do. I was willing to show her how to get out, but she was terrified. This doesn't excuse her behavior. What she did was wrong. But you can leave the judging of your mom's heart to Me."

Callie knew what she needed to do, but releasing these things was so hard. "Jesus, help me to let this go. Help me to trust You." Again, they repeated the words together. She opened her eyes but still felt like running away.

"Listen," said Raymond, "I know this is so hard for you to still be dealing with, but I see people every week that are going through the same types of memories, who have experienced the same type of abuse. Your father was most likely involved in a secret society, much like the lodge next to the long-standing church downtown. This kind of extreme abuse happens way more than people want to admit."

Callie sighed heavily and nodded. She could let her mom go and trust her to Jesus.

But Raymond said, "Callie, there's something else, isn't there? I see your legs going a mile a minute. What's going on?"

"I don't know." Her teeth were chattering. "I feel terrified. Like I'm going to lose my mind again."

"Let's ask Jesus where you should go now."

Callie nodded blankly and closed her eyes.

Not again. She heard screaming in her head, violent screaming, as the final seal broke. *You'll die. You can't see this.*

"I didn't die back then." Callie repeated words she had heard Raymond say. "It will be OK. Please, let me see this."

In the black of the summer night, the only light she saw was a fire blazing in the distance over ancient mounds. "I am a god," a hooded figure claimed. "Obey me." He forced drugs down her throat in spite of her gagging struggle against them. He shoved a white hood over her head so that she viewed the night's events from behind eye holes.

Then she saw her brother and sisters beside her, bound like sheep for the slaughter.

"If you don't do exactly as we say, we'll murder them." The hooded man grabbed Callie and assaulted her. Rage filled her heart, and the hooded man immediately tried to use that rage against her by forcing a knife into her hand, commanding her to take part.

I'm like them. I've become like them. I've become the dragon.

The night wore on as covenants were made with Satan and promises were repeated that if the story were ever told, she and her family would be murdered in cold blood.

She repeated the frightful words. That was the night she didn't try to escape. That was the night the lies were sealed in her heart.

A coming of age, she thought bitterly.

A baby was placed in young Callie's arms, still alive, but barely. She held the child against her breast, following the leader down a winding path through dark woods. In the distance, she could hear the sound of gurgling water.

"Get down in the river." In the darkness, she distinguished that she and her little sister had been brought to the edge of the bank.

"Get down in the water now, and dispose of it."

"No. I won't." The baby was limp in her arms but she could feel its shallow breathing "She's alive. I can't."

"Then it will be your sister's life instead." The shadow grabbed her sister from behind, holding a knife to her throat.

"I have no choice." Callie muttered to herself. Tears streamed down her face as she stepped into the water. "I have no choice."

She held the child in the water as the last life slipped away, releasing the body to float downstream.

I'm a murderer. I have become like my father.

Callie looked up to see both Greg and Raymond with tears in their eyes from the scene she had been describing.

"Callie, I'm so very sorry." Greg's voice cracked. "I can't imagine. I didn't know."

"I deserve to die." Her voice sounded hollow, distant, like it belonged to someone else.

"No, Callie." Raymond spoke gently. "Any child in this circumstance would have done the same thing."

"I feel like I need to turn myself in."

"If you were to do that, there is no court of law that would hold you accountable." Raymond leaned forward. "I am speaking the truth to you. You did not become like your father. These were manipulative lies to get you to do what these wicked men wanted you to do. You only listened and obeyed those you thought were in authority over you. Any child would have done what you did. Those men are held responsible before God. They gave into hate and lies. You didn't. Satan himself is not strong enough to take you out of God's hands. Nothing can separate you from God's love."

Callie shook her head in disbelief. The lies had penetrated so deep. "I can't ask Jesus to come here. It's too horrible."

"Is there any place too evil for Him to go? Any place too painful, too hurtful that He can't heal? Any darkness too dark for Him to penetrate? He loves you, Callie. Let Him in."

Finally she whispered the words, in desperation.

Immediately, brilliant light penetrated the darkness. There in Jesus' arms she saw the young child, the one she had just been holding, but it was alive. Then she saw Jesus hand the child to an angelic being, who took the child to heaven. Jesus turned back towards her with eyes of compassion. He lifted the hood off her head and kissed her on the cheek.

"My dear child. My dear, precious child." He held her in His everlasting arms and wept with her. Then He commanded another angel to bring her new clothes, gently asking her if He could clean her up and reclothe her. She nodded. When they were done, she was dazzling white like He was.

After they had forgiven, Jesus asked her, "What do you believe about yourself?" She told him the lies she had believed as truth.

"Dear, dear child. You never for a moment became like your father. They tried to force it upon you, but even the rage you felt was righteous anger. I felt the same anger when I witnessed their rebellious, hideous sins. I understand, dear one. But I also see your heart, and who you really are. You never became like one of them, because you said yes to Me. I've kept you safe in my love since that day. There is nothing they could do to force you to turn. Nothing. And that baby is now with Me forever. I don't hold that against you, dear one. Don't hold this against yourself. Will you choose to believe Me?"

The question hung suspended for what seemed an eternity.

"I choose to believe you, Jesus." Callie looked up into His beautiful face. All she found there was pure love like she'd never known before. A seed of joy was planted in her heart.

"Then let's dance on injustice." He took her by the hand and twirled her right over the blood-stained ground, as all heaven and hell watched.

As the dance slowed, He spoke to her again. "Callie, you may have to forgive them a thousand times. Are you willing to do that?"

She gripped His precious scarred hands.

"Yes, Lord. A thousand times."

CHAPTER 18

Callie, teen years

Madison, Indiana

Now Callie bore the responsibility of raising her brother and sisters as well as most of the household duties. But it was the weight of their circumstances that bore down the heaviest.

In the middle of her freshman year of high school, the heavy load became too much to bear. That day her best friend Rey slipped her a note. "Last night I had sex for the first time, with my new boyfriend."

As Callie read that note, everything crumbled inside her. She didn't go back to school for the rest of the year. Every time she tried to set foot out the front door of their small house, she vomited.

"Callie, what is it? What's wrong?" Mama pressed for answers. But Callie had no idea. She didn't know why the note from Rey had been the last straw breaking her, the last drip that tipped everything over.

Hoping for answers, Mama took her from doctor to psychologist to doctor. But no one helped her get better, and some of them made her worse. One doctor examined her and then bluntly asked, "Are you a virgin?"

"Yes," Callie answered. She truly believed it. In her fragmented mind, there was no memory of anything else.

"No, you're not." His words were scornful, almost as if he were spitting.

Callie turned hot and red with embarrassment and humiliation. *How could he have said that? What could he have meant?* Quickly she dressed herself and shoved his words away.

Hopelessness set into her family, like an open, festering wound. Often in the evenings after work, Mama came home with bruises on her face. "Oh, I ran into a door at work," she would say. "Everybody says I'm the clumsiest person there."

But one morning, when Callie was sitting beside Mama on her bed, Mama told the truth.

"I'm beating myself," she said. "I hate my life. I wish I were dead."

Callie was stunned, not knowing what to say. Here was one more burden for her to carry.

She had thought it was bad when her father had been around. But maybe this existence was even worse.

⁎)+ℳ

School began again, but nothing in Callie could make herself go back for her sophomore year. Instead, she hid trapped behind the four walls of their small house each day, while her sisters and brother hustled off to catch the bus and Mama wearily left for work.

"Callie Mae, be sure to get the clothes washed and dried before I get home. I need my work clothes ready."

"Yes, ma'am. I'll get it done."

Bleakness seeped in like cold air through the cracks of the 85-year-old house Mama had been able to afford. Temperatures dropped swiftly that fall.

Lonely and cold, Callie spent each day in a prison of her own making.

She observed how hollow the living room felt, with the only items in it an old sofa they had found at the Goodwill, the rocking chair her Mama had rocked her in when she was a little girl, and the record player.

She walked over to it, sitting in the corner there with *The Sound of Music* record spinning around.

Oh, she could remember her Mama gathering them up in her arms when they were little, all snuggled together in her bed during storms, quietly singing "My Favorite Things."

Unconsciously, Callie began humming the tune, trying to offer herself some comfort. But the needle was tapping the side of the record's plastic rim.

Callie pushed the black switch to off. The songs were over.

Mama did the best she could. *Focus on today, Callie. Just focus on today.* Callie could learn to trust God just for today, the way Mama did with groceries.

Every week, Mama took Callie to the welfare office and waited in the car while Callie had to go stand in line to get a big jar of peanut butter, a block of processed cheese, and a couple of loaves of bread. Every week Callie stood in that long line, head down, not saying a word, her face bright red with shame. But each week the needs of the family were fulfilled.

ဆာလ

Finally one day Mama said, "Callie, you've got to go back to school after Christmas. I know it's hard, honey, but you've got to start putting one foot in front of the other. Don't look back, even if you're scared. You can't just quit school. You have to try."

"But Mama, I can't. I just can't. I start to gag when I even step out of the front door. How am I supposed to go back to school?"

Callie was also keenly aware that she would have to face the allegation of a teen pregnancy. Rey had told her the stories that had spread like wildfire when she hadn't returned.

"Daughter, you have no choice in this. You will just have to try."

The New Year came, and Mama finally persuaded Callie to get dressed for school and get in the car. She drove to the front of the enormous high school building, practically pushing Callie out.

"If you need to, go to the nurse's office and take a break, but you're going to have to stay."

Full of anxiety, Callie wiped the tears from her eyes, waved goodbye, and reluctantly walked into the building.

She slunk into the cafeteria to pick up her free lunch ticket, which she had done since in kindergarten. The older she got, the more humiliating it was. But the lady behind the register just smiled at her, greeting her with a kind, "Good morning, sweetheart."

Callie ducked back into the hall to find her locker. Turn, click, turn backwards, click, turn frontwards again, click. *Praise God, it works.* She was off to her homeroom, sliding into her desk before the bell rang. Most people were new, and no one spoke of the reason of her absence, not even Rey.

The first two weeks, she spent at least one class period a day in the nurse's office, like Mama had told her, but with each passing day, her confidence grew, until the need to escape passed. Even gym class proved a confidence-building experience rather than being full of embarrassment. The class focused on weights, aerobics, and learning how to care for your body, all of which helped Callie begin to pull out of the depression that had held her underwater.

During that time Mama began bringing home one man after another. *Trying them out, I suppose.* One was a hippie guy who smoked weed, another a well-dressed business man. Then there was the blue-collar redneck with a beer belly. And finally, there was Rich, a Pentecostal Holiness Christian that Mama had met while working as a waitress. With his baby face and chin covered in peace fuzz for a beard, he looked more like Callie's older brother than Mama's boyfriend.

৪৩৫৪

One afternoon in May Callie placed a letter in Mama's hands. It was from Me-Ma and Paw-Paw.

Dear Cheryl,

We'd like to invite Callie to come and spend the summer with us. Please consider it. Bring the other kids for a few days for a vacation for yourself. Hope to see you soon.

Love,

Mom

Callie's heart leaped with hope. "Please, Mama, please, can I go?" She tried not to sound too desperate, but she was dying to go, especially now that Me-Ma and Paw-Paw had moved from the flatlands of Florida to the rolling mountains of Tennessee.

"I need you here," said Mama. "I can't get along without you. What will I do with your brother and sisters over the summer? Who will watch them?"

"Eva's thirteen now, Mama. I was watching them when I was younger than that! She can do it. I need to go. Please." *I have to get away for a while.*

And to her relief, Mama finally relented. Callie got to go.

At Me-Ma and Paw-Paw's house, for the first time since Pops and Tucker, Callie felt completely safe and fully loved.

In the mornings, she meandered behind Me-Ma to the flourishing garden, the dew still glistening like diamonds on the grass, soaking her toes through her sandals. Tomatoes in red bunches, squash, gigantic cucumbers, zucchini, okra, string beans, corn, and herbs were all ripe and ready to be picked.

Callie filled her baskets, her cheeks, and the front of her shirt. Then she went back out to pick the raspberries and blueberries that lined the yard.

Once a week she went out with Paw-Paw to pick wild blackberries, and Me-Ma made delectable blackberry cobbler. Callie had never been any place that seemed so close to heaven.

Then Me-Ma taught her how to paint.

"I think you'd do a great job at this, Callie," she said. "It's called tole painting. The acrylics are over here. Here, take this decoration out to the porch table and see what happens."

Callie was entranced. Gathering together all the supplies, she spread out to begin painting, and she didn't stop for the rest of the summer. Me-Ma supplied her with old saws, then t-shirts, and finally canvases.

Callie loved painting the mountains best. Looking up, she could see the mountain directly in front and hear the music of the stream bubbling along below.

Brush stroke after brush stroke, Callie painted into the late afternoon most days, until the smell of dinner cooking brought her back to the present.

In the evenings, they all gathered on the deck and talked over the day's activities. Often, Paw-Paw picked up a tune he had learned as a young man in the navy, silly tunes of girls named Sally sitting under the cherry tree. She knew the words were often made up as he sang, adding to the amusement.

As the sun fully set, the sky grew black and the stars came out in full measure. Callie lingered here in the coolness of night, flipping her head back to watch for shooting stars.

But she knew it couldn't last. The time came when Mama returned to get her.

Though Callie left her grandparents' house with as much compliance as possible, still she felt trapped in the car with Mama on one side and Rich on the other. Suddenly she burst into tears. "Please, Mama, please. I want to go back and live with Me-Ma and Paw-Paw. Please."

But no matter how she begged, Mama remained unmoved. "It's time for us to make a new family now, Callie. I'm going to marry Rich. You're a part of this family, and you are not going back."

Finally Callie wiped her tears, determined she would never shed another tear in front of her mother again.

※※※

The first Sunday Callie visited Rich's Pentecostal Holiness Church, Mama took her up front for prayer. There in the front of the auditorium she felt cornered like a frightened mouse as a crowd of strangers laid their hands on her. They prayed loudly and feverishly, calling on the Holy Spirit and speaking strange words.

Dad always said the Holy Ghost isn't for today. He said people who speak in tongues are of the devil. I gotta get out of here. Callie frantically sought a way of escape, but saw none. Her body shook as the blood drained from her face. She was afraid she was going to faint.

After that, it took many weeks for Callie to even be willing to go back into the regular church service again, but she did finally attend a youth meeting. "So glad to have you, Callie!" the youth pastors said. "We're having Bible studies at our house. Want to come?"

Sure, I'd love an excuse to escape my place.

It wasn't long before she began to love these people and make new friends. At the weekend youth conference, when the speaker invited the young people to come receive the Holy Spirit, one of Callie's new friends pushed her into the aisle and down front. When Callie asked the Lord to give her the Holy Spirit, her body felt as if it were on fire with the warmth of God's love.

Callie, we're beginning a new friendship with each other. She could feel the voice rather than hear Him. *I'll never leave you or forsake you.*

For the first time in her life, she knew she'd never be alone again.

But the more Callie connected with the people at church, the less she felt like she belonged at home. Rich demanded all of Mama's attention, and Mama readily gave it. When he said they needed to move again, Mama agreed.

But his plan was to move in with Me-Ma and Paw-Paw.

That lasted a week.

"He's a spoiled, rotten, good for nothing. . . ." She could hear Paw-Paw's booming voice echoing through the walls. "If he sets another foot in this house, I'll fill him up with the lead from my rifle!"

But while the rest of the family camped all summer, homeless and penniless, Callie managed to finagle her way to stay with Me-Ma and Paw-Paw for the whole summer again. When fall came, she found new friends at her new school and spent as much time with them as possible.

But Rich grew restless and decided to pick up and move yet again.

Lord, what's wrong with me? Do You never want me to have friends who love me? Is it because I love them too much? Are You punishing me?

No, child. But this is not where you need to be.

Little did she know it then, but when they moved for the final time, her senior year of high school, that was where she would meet Greg ten years later.

CHAPTER 19

A Fresh Start

(Spring 1994)

The Sunday before their pastor announced his departure, leaving behind half of an already dwindling congregation, God had already spoken to Greg about their next church home.

"When we visit there, I just sense they're so hungry for God," Greg said. "They seem so sincere. So on fire." It was clear this new church family was where they needed to be.

Callie sighed. "My heart is broken for the people at our old church, though. I don't understand why they can't just forgive each other and work things out, when I've had to forgive so much." She struggled to make sense of it all, and she deeply felt the loss of friendships she had held onto throughout the last ten years.

"But you can't control people, Cal. You can't make them forgive. I really think you'll like our new church family."

Greg pushed her toward the new place, the new connections. "Besides, Mary and Danny are already there."

That did give her hope.

ഗ്രക്ക

"Greg, do you remember Aira? She's the one I saw dancing my freedom, you know, the day I saw that first awful memory. She invited me to come to a prayer group at her house."

Uncertainty filled Callie's voice. "But I can't pray for anybody else when I'm so messed up still myself."

"Maybe you should give it a try," Greg encouraged her. "You can invite Mary to come with you."

Trust was something that came with great, great effort, but Callie had already taken a huge step of trust in telling Mary the nasty details of her story a few months earlier. Mary hadn't closed her eyes or turned away from her. Instead, she had pressed in more to their friendship.

Mary had chosen to love her, even when Callie had allowed herself to be fully known. Because how can you really know if someone loves you, until you are fully known by them?

To be fully known takes great courage. Perhaps, it is the greatest courage. But true love has no fear of being fully known.

The next Tuesday morning, Callie cautiously entered Aira's home, finding a seat on the floor near the door. Mary showed up a little late, but gave her a quick wink.

Callie stared at the carpet, shifting her legs around on the floor. When they went around the room introducing themselves, she wanted to hide. *I don't belong here.*

But something about Aira drew Callie to her. After the prayer time, she decided to jump hurdles of fear. "I feel like I'm fighting with God," she confided.

Aira's only advice came abruptly. "Then wrestle with Him well. He can handle it."

That's no help. She doesn't understand me. Wrestle with God. All I want is someone to fix me. Callie left frustrated, wanting answers, not a wrestling match.

Week after week, Callie showed up for the prayer group. "I don't feel qualified to be in a prayer group like this," she confessed to Mary. "I don't even know what I'm doing. I still have all these crazy thoughts I'm fighting all the time."

"I don't know what I'm doing either, but it's a lot of fun." Mary's jovial laugh always made Callie feel better, lessening the cloud that still hovered over her head.

Before long, the prayer group began meeting in the church fellowship hall, which made Callie even more uncomfortable. It was October, and the cold had set in.

"Callie, I want you to take a group back to the corner of the property and pray together there." As the words left Aira's mouth, Callie's heart began to beat wildly.

"Excuse me?"

"You take a group to the back corner and pray," Aira repeated. "I'll take a group to the other corner. Mary, you'll take the corner closest to the road."

Mary shot Callie a concerned look.

Going outside in the dark behind a church didn't sound like a great idea, but Callie tried to rehearse reassurance to her mind. *It will be OK. I'll be OK.*

A group gathered as she led the way.

This is silly. Why am I so afraid? In her gut, she knew why.

They entered the blackness of the cloudy night, stumbling their way back past the playground, with only a single flashlight to guide them. As they came to the back corner of the property, the group stood huddled together, trying to keep warm. Callie zipped up her jacket and pulled it around her neck as the October chill seeped in.

Quietly, they all listened for words, scriptures, or images they might hear in their hearts to pray. Each got a piece of what to pray as the Spirit spoke to their hearts. One by one, they spoke out their petitions.

Callie's heart slowed to a thump, thump.

Timidly, the last one spoke up. Callie had met this young woman once before, but she hadn't said a word in the group, up until now. The young woman started to pray, slowly at first, but ending on a note of confidence. As the sound of her voice frosted the night air, a cold wind whipped up.

As they returned to the building, the small woman, whose prayers had seemingly evoked the wind, approached Callie. Twinkling hazel green eyes pierced through the darkness, and a compassionate smile spread across her face. "I just wanted to introduce myself. My name is Monica."

As she warmly hugged the chill off of Callie, Callie could feel in her bones that their hearts would be woven together.

ಙ೦ಚ

Come.

It was 5:30 in the summer morning, at the beach house where Callie and Greg and their children were vacationing with Mary's family. Thirteen people and barely a moment to think a quiet thought.

Except at 5:30 in the morning, when the Lord called her.

Sleepily, she climbed out of bed, slipped on her flip flops, and headed out the door to watch the sunrise on the horizon. Each time, God met her there.

Tomorrow, I want to you to come, and you are going to throw some things in the sea.

That seems strange, Lord.

The next morning at 5:30 as she walked, she heard, *Daughter, I will never leave you. Today I want you to pick up the stones I show you and let them represent your fears and the lies you still believe about yourself.*

As Callie continued, she noticed small black stones she hadn't noticed before. She picked up seven and held them loosely in the palm of her hands, turning the smooth stones with her fingers.

Now, name them and throw them into the sea of My love.

"But Lord, they may roll back."

No, in the sea of My love they will be lost forever.

She obeyed, naming each rock for each fear or lie she still believed, tossing them one by one into the frothy, crashing waves. As the tide rolled out, the stones tumbled over and over, being carried further and further out to sea, until Callie could no longer see them.

As she threw the last stone, seagulls flew overhead.

Daughter, I want you to fly now.

"How can I do that, Lord?"

A gentle answer drifted into her mind as if on the wind.

How does a bird fly? They are weak, small creatures that can be crushed in a human's hand, yet they soar high, defying gravity. They do what they were created for. So, you are created to fly. You are created to fly high. Look at Me. It's OK to be vulnerable. You are safe here. It's OK to feel love, to be loved.

You aren't going to hurt anyone. I want you to have fun in life and be like a little child with her good Daddy. You're no longer a slave to fear. You are a child of God! So, fly!

Callie pondered the words she had heard as she returned to the beach house.

That evening Greg and Callie had their turn for an evening out, just the two of them. They walked hand in hand to the end of the pier with the cool evening breeze blowing through Callie's long hair.

Greg glanced over at his bride. "Callie, I'm so glad you were the one God chose for me."

Surprised, Callie's face grew red. "Oh, Greg. I still don't understand why He chose me. I'm so sorry for the long, hard road you've had to walk with me."

"Sweetheart, you're worth it."

They stood silently at the end of the pier watching the sunset.

A new day is coming, dear one. I have so many good things in store for you both.

Callie didn't argue this time, but rested back into Greg's shoulder as he leaned over gently to kiss her.

Later that evening Mary came out to Callie, who lay swinging on the hammock. "Brought you something."

Callie reached out to receive the thick slice of watermelon. Its juice dripped off her chin as she sank her teeth into the goodness.

Jesus, you are good. Thank You for showing me.

80C3

As counseling went on, bits and pieces of her story continued to be unearthed, but also they began to make sense. Like a great puzzle coming together, God kept on turning pages, re-vealing truth, and putting her mind back together. It became smoother and smoother.

It never became easier to look at, but easier to receive the truth, and the truth was taking hold.

The largest wounds had been exposed and were beginning to heal from the inside out. Callie could finally breathe a little.

"Will there ever be an end to this?" she asked Raymond.

"Yes, Callie. One day you'll be fully at peace, because all the pain will have been dealt with." Raymond firmly believed that. Callie wanted to, but it still seemed like every time she walked out the door of his office, something else would come up.

But the hurricane was abating. Though she could still see wind, rain, and surge, it was far less intense.

As she left that evening, Raymond opened his arms for an approving hug, and she melted into his fatherly embrace. "Callie, I am so proud of you, little girl. You are becoming whole. I couldn't be happier with you."

Raymond patted Greg on the back as well. "You too, buddy. Greg, I'm proud of you too. Well done being a good husband to Callie."

Even if it might not have been the last chapter of the book, it felt like things were coming to a close.

CHAPTER 20

Callie, young adult
Atlanta, Georgia

Callie's car idled in the parking lot of the large Christian school as she read through her résumé for the hundredth time. She glanced up to watch a child in uniform walk through the doors. *So happy and confident.*

Only a few weeks earlier, shortly after her college graduation, Mama had gotten that infamous anonymous letter saying Callie's father's sins had finally caught up with him. He had been convicted of being a sexual predator. *A pedophile.*

Finally.

Can't think about that now. Got to focus.

"O God, help me. I'm so nervous about getting this job." She breathed in deeply. Then before she could chicken out, she jumped out of the car, nearly slamming the door of her small Ford.

"Sorry, old friend." She patted the hood before making her way to the door.

"It's good to meet you, Callie. Come in and have a seat." The middle-aged woman, kindly but professional, motioned for her to sit opposite her immaculate desk. The name plate in the center prominently displayed, "Principal Dr. Kathy Wellborn."

Callie tucked her skirt under her as she scooted closer to the door.

Only a few steps to the exit. Good. We'll be fine. Just breathe.

"Your résumé looks good," Dr. Wellborn said, peering at Callie over her glasses.

"Thank you. I'm really excited about the possibility of working here." Callie glanced back at the door, but quickly turned to face her potential new boss.

Try to look calm. Keep eye contact. We need this job.

"So, where are you from?" Mrs. Wellborn said.

"Oh, I've lived lots of places, but my family moved here about five years ago, before I went off to college."

"I see. Job transfer?"

"Um. My mom wanted to live closer to her parents." Callie wiggled a little in her seat, wanting to change the subject quickly. "You have my résumé there. See, that's where I went to college, and my volunteer work there has prepared me for teaching."

Dr. Wellborn drew her eyes back to the résumé, where they belonged. "We do need a first-grade teacher next year," she said, "but I have one other promising person also interviewing for this position."

Callie nodded her head in agreement. *They'll pick someone else. She can tell I'm nervous. Probably thinks I'm stupid.*

"Let me take you for a tour of the school to meet some of the children."

They walked through the narrow hallways, and she opened one of the doors. "This is Ms. Gail's kindergarten class."

Callie saw colorful bulletin boards and children scattered around noisily chattering while coloring their assignment. In the middle, bringing order to the chaos, stood a slender, tall woman with dark skin and curly hair. As she looked up to see who had just interrupted, her eyes met Callie's with a twinkle and a grin from ear to ear.

I've got to get to know that woman. I don't know why, but I do.

Ms. Gail was introduced to Callie at the door. "So, this will be your class next year, Ms. Callie," she said. "If you're brave enough to take up the challenge." She laughed, patting Callie on the shoulder. Callie's stomach fluttered.

ഃറ൘

Every morning since starting her new job, Callie had to rush to use the toilet before the first bell rang. The children were usually already settled before she entered.

But as the weeks rolled by, the urges to escape the room lessened.

Ms. Gail was right about the challenge of this class, that's for sure.

"So, how has your day been?" Gail asked later in the break room. "Are you adjusting well? That's a tough class."

Callie slipped off her dress shoe and rubbed her heel. "I didn't realize teaching was so tiring."

Gail gave her a knowing nod. "I'm really glad you came to work here. It's good to have a new friend."

"Well, you made me feel comfortable from the day I came. I still remember your cheesy smile." Callie hesitated. "And you seem to know everyone around here."

"Well, I've been here for a while." Gail winked.

A burst of bravery rose up in Callie. "Do you happen to know the guy who showed up yesterday to help at the desk with the accounting? I thought he was kind of cute."

"You mean the blond guy with the fuzzy mustache?" Gail said. "Actually, he works downtown with my husband at his accounting firm. And yes, I saw that he doesn't have a ring on his finger."

She patted Callie's hand. "You just leave it to me. I'll find out who he is."

ৡেওঙ্গ

A few weeks later, Gail pulled Callie to the side after school. "His name is Greg McCormick. He's single. We're going to set you up on a date."

Set her up she did. On Friday when school ended, Callie rushed out her door with a pile of papers to grade, but she failed to see the man standing on the other side. As she slammed into him, papers flew into the air.

"Oh, I'm sorry. I didn't see you." Callie bent over to grab her work off the floor. Greg quickly follow suit. She muttered awkward thanks as he handed her the last of them. *My cheeks feel like they're on fire.*

"Hey, um. My name is Greg. Gail said I should meet you." Gail was standing behind him, with a hand on his back.

"Callie, this is Greg. Greg, Callie. I'll be going now." She had that grin on her face.

Callie shot her a look of "Thanks a lot, friend." But then she politely said to Greg, "Well, uh, Gail said you work with her husband."

"Yeah. He's actually a good friend of mine." Greg held the door for her as they headed for the parking lot together. Something about his presence made Callie breathe easier.

He cleared his throat. "You wanna grab some dinner and talk a little? Not like a date or anything. I'm not into dating girls right now."

Not into dating girls?

Callie's quizzical look caused Greg's face to grow crimson. "Hmm. I like girls. I mean women. Oh." His face grew redder and redder, as if it was about to pop. Then he hung his head. "I don't have a good history in dating. I always screw stuff up."

"It's OK. I've not dated a lot anyway. Let's not call it a date. But a talk would be nice."

౹౦౦౩

I've got to tell him about my family. About my dad. He's got to know. And when he finds out, that will be the end. Just like in every other relationship I've had. Better to drop the bomb now, rather than have my heart crushed like the last guy who took off.

As she waited for Greg to pick her up for their Saturday hiking trip, Callie paced the floor of her apartment. *He's got to know. I can't lie to him. Besides, if he researches my family he'll find out what kind of man my dad is.*

As they walked down the secluded dirt trail, they came to a place beside a small creek where they could sit.

What am I thinking? This is so isolated. I don't like this at all. How far is it back to the car?

"Callie, are you OK?" Greg asked. "You seem a little tense. The backpack too heavy for you?"

"No, no." Callie slowly sat down on a rock, ready to drop the bomb. "There's something you need to know about my family."

Greg easily sat down next to her. "Sounds serious. What's on your mind?"

She stared at the ground and twisted her fingers. "My dad was convicted of pedophilia." Then she looked up quickly to offer reassurance. "He—he never did things to me. I was like in a bubble. But he abused other kids. We found out after my parents divorced."

"Wow." Greg thought for a moment, and then looked Callie straight in the eyes. "Callie, everyone's family has issues. Mine was my mom. She controlled everything I ever did. But the past is the past. It doesn't affect our future."

"Really, you believe that?"

"Yes. I really do. Trust me on this." He reached out for her hand and held it gently.

Tingly warmth flowed through her body, awakening feelings long forgotten.

ഇര

"Hey, Gail. Let's grab a burger and a coke before we head home today. I'm hungry." Callie was good at stalling her friend in getting home.

"Let me give Ken a call first and make sure."

Callie could tell from the nod that Ken was working late again with Greg. "I'll see you when you get home, babe."

As they got in the car, Callie said, "Gail, what's it like to have a happy marriage? I've never seen one."

"Oh, we have our ups and downs and disagreements, but on the whole it's a beautiful thing." Gail paused. "And would you happen to be thinking about marriage?"

Callie blushed and didn't reply.

At the fast-food place, Callie got in line, but Gail held back. Several white men stood between them.

"Gail, come up here and get in line with me. We're together."

Gail just shook her head and looked down, pretending not to notice.

Not getting the hint, Callie persisted, "Come on. It's fine."

Gail shot her a look that said, "Shut up, before you get me hung."

Callie relented, but when they were walking out, she cornered her friend. "That wasn't like you. What was wrong?"

"Callie, I'm black, remember. You're white. They could have killed me for getting in front of them," Gail said. "You don't understand. How could you?"

But deep down, something in Callie did understand, and her chest began to ache.

ဆဝၗ

Not many months later, Callie was one of several friends and relatives keeping vigil in the sterile hospital halls where Gail lay dying of cancer.

"Are you Callie?" It was the nurse. "She wants to see you."

"But I can't go into ICU."

"She says you're her sister."

Pushing back the curtain, Callie collapsed in tears next to her friend.

"Callie, look at me. Please, look at me." Gail waited until their eyes met. "Callie, listen to me. The cancer has gone through my whole body. It's in my bones. They aren't giving me much time to live, maybe not even a day."

Callie hid her face in her hands. "What? No. That can't be true."

"Sweetheart, I want you to know this. Before this year is up, you will marry that man out there, Greg McCormick. When you do, I'll be dancing at your wedding."

Gail died that night in her sleep.

CHAPTER 21

Victory March

(Spring 1996)

What am I doing here? Am I out of my ever-loving mind?

I'm going to open the door of this truck and jump out on the highway.

No, no I'm not. I'll sit on my hands so I can't.

"Callie, you OK?" Monica, the new friend from prayer group, was driving.

"Uh, yeah," Callie muttered. "It's just been a long time since I've been to a women's retreat."

"Not a great experience, huh?"

How can Monica read me so well?

"No, not exactly." Callie laughed nervously. "It was twelve years ago, but . . . let's just say I had an overzealous roommate. Wanted to know too much about me."

Monica nodded slowly, knowingly. "This time you got a roommate who'll let you stay with Mary the whole time if you want to."

Callie smiled at her friend's understanding response. That evening, she tucked herself safely next to Mary as the first session of the retreat began.

As the music swelled, Aira, the prayer group leader, began a dance she had choreographed herself.

Callie leaned over and whispered in Mary's ear. "Aira once danced my freedom."

"What do you mean?"

"The first time I saw a ritual memory, she was the one in the sanctuary dancing. I had peeked in to watch, and that was the first time I ever saw her."

Now Aira was dancing her freedom again. Callie was so completely captivated by the words, the music, and the movements that she had to remind herself to breathe.

But when the speaker got up to talk, Callie knew she was in trouble. Right away she heard the Father's voice.

Callie, you're afraid of intimacy with Me as your Father. You don't really trust Me yet.

Well, yeah. Of course I don't. I know Jesus, that He's safe, but how can I trust you as my Father? Fathers aren't safe. A bubble of rage rose in her chest. Desperately she tried to push it back down, but she felt like she had been kicked in the gut, hard.

The speaker wove a story into her talk about her own healing journey through abuse.

And for the first time, Callie realized that in all her memories she had never seen God as a Father. In fact, as she tried to visualize herself climbing onto the Father's lap, all she saw was Him abusing her.

Panic and lightheadedness overtook her as she looked for ways to escape the crowded room. *Where are the exits?*

Help me. I can't do this. I can't do this now. Not here. Not now.

I'm not in a safe place. I don't have it in me to do this.

A new bubble was beginning to burst, and all she could see was ugly coming out.

Callie, come to the prayer room and offer this to Me.

Quickly she stumbled out to obey the voice speaking to her heart. On her knees she wept as she tried to find a place of surrender.

"Callie, you are not going down." This time the voice was behind her. "You are going to a higher place."

It was Mary, who had followed her in to pray with her.

"Come on. You can do this."

෨෦෬

As morning broke, Callie heard in her heart, *Today, you will build Me an altar.*

She hated altars. When she saw them in her mind, she saw the little children on them . . . and herself.

Why me, to build You an altar? That seems very mean of You, Father, who I am supposed to be learning to trust. How could You ask me to do that? Build an altar for You?

As she walked outside, she slowed her pace to a stop. There in front of her, a flashback of a memory lit up the screen of her mind.

She was a little three-year-old girl again, her hands and feet tied tightly, as she suffered on a table.

Time stood still. She heard Jesus speak.

Callie, I took your place, and while I took what they gave you, Abba was holding you. As you were dying, I asked you if you would be willing to stay on earth so that you could one day help others. And you said yes to Me. It was the Father who held your quaking little broken body and breathed the breath of life back into your limp lungs.

The realization completely stunned her. She grabbed the metal railing next to her. "O God." She took a deep breath, trying to steady herself as tears welled up in her eyes.

As the morning session began and music filled the room, Callie again slipped into a vision.

She saw herself laboring to build a stone altar. Her knuckles were bloody and raw, her strength almost completely spent.

Then Jesus approached her, humming a tune and smiling. "May I help you build this, sweetheart?"

"Yes, please," she said.

As He began picking up the rough stones and putting them into place in the altar, He whistled. The heaviness of the task lifted, and it was completed in no time.

Callie turned towards her Lord. "What are the stones, Jesus?"

"Your memories."

"What must I sacrifice?"

"Praise."

Oh, praise. Praise for all the times He has met me. Praise for all the times He has wept with me, holding me. For all the times He showed me His wounded hands and feet to prove it was really Him. Praise for making something beautiful out of my broken mess.

The sweetness of the moment swept over her. She curled into a ball with the music flowing over her like a stream.

৺ঙ

For weeks before the retreat, Callie had awoken at 4:43 am. That afternoon, as the clock neared 4:30, she determined to go to the prayer garden down the pebbled path.

There she saw a stone table that looked like it could have been where Aslan had offered himself in Narnia.

Sitting down on the damp, mossy slab, she simply asked, "What now, Papa?"

Papa. That word felt weird rolling off her lips.

Sing a song of thanks to Me.

A song of praise softly rose from her broken heart.

"Thank you, Papa, for never leaving me. Thank you for healing my broken heart. To the best of my ability, I lay down the fear of intimacy. I belong to You."

On the last morning of the retreat, Callie awoke at the familiar time of 4:43 a.m. As she fully gained her senses, His voice came again. *I want to seal this with a kiss.*

It was time to drive to the top of the mountain. And Monica would go with her.

As the hazy sky was awaking, the two friends climbed into the truck and rode to the top of the mountain to watch the sunrise over the peaks. Pinks, reds, oranges, and deep blues gave way to the blazing ball of fire that pierced the horizon with brilliance.

There they basked in the rays of His love, offering Papa thanksgiving for His goodness. They drank in every moment as a sweet new wine.

As they slowly walked back to the truck down the old gravel road, Monica pointed. "Look, Callie!"

The sign read "New Adventure Trails."

"Wow," said Callie. "I wonder what new adventures Papa has in store for us."

ഇൟ

Callie, come on a walk with me this morning. Come watch the sun rise.

The women's retreat was far behind her. Callie was growing more and more used to listening to the voice of her Papa now. She climbed out of bed quietly, careful not to wake Greg.

Pulling on a jacket over her sweat pants and t-shirt, she tucked her hair into her ball cap.

Papa knew what was on her heart today.

A few months earlier she had found out that not only had Monica grown up in the Ohio River Valley, not far from the site of the last ritual they had done on Callie, but that Monica's grandfather had actually taken her to those very grounds when she was a young girl.

As Callie walked and pondered in the dim light of early dawn, she felt a gentle nudge towards a nearby field. She turned to walk in that direction.

Together Monica and Callie had determined that they would go back to the Ohio River Valley, to offer prayers of forgiveness and blessing. Monica was excited. Greg was supportive.

Callie had a knot in her stomach.

It feels like God is asking me to be like Abraham bringing Isaac to be sacrificed. Her words to Monica echoed in her head. *Except I'm the one being offered up.*

Yeah, preachers' kids were always living sacrifices, weren't they? Callie wrestled with that memory as her sneakers padded quietly on the road.

The Lord gently reminded her of the truth.

Callie, I provided the lamb in the thicket for Abraham. I already became the perfect sacrifice for you. No other sacrifice is needed.

The sky morphed rapidly through soft purples and pinks. She would need to hurry if she was going to get to the field by sunrise.

They had chosen the date, September 17th, the day on the Jewish calendar when forgiveness for the wrongs of the past year are asked and granted. And 17 represented complete victory.

It had all been settled. They were going to the Ohio River Valley.

Until Raymond had surprised them by advising against it. Monica had then acknowledged that she felt they didn't have to go so far to offer these prayers, that they could do it from here.

"What do you want me to do now, Papa?" Callie muttered, kicking a stone. "Why are you making me choose? You know I hate making decisions, especially ones this big." She just wanted to obey a command. It was so much easier that way. And September 17th was just a few days away now.

Callie.

Her senses awakened to the sweet presence, and she looked up to see the open field before her.

How do you want to see the sun rise, dear one? Would you like to view it from the open field or from the covered area beside the trees?

You're giving me a choice?

Callie looked out at the field. She knew it would soon grow too warm there, and people passing would have full view of her. She longed for privacy.

Turning towards the covered area, she found a comfortable spot where she could watch the blazing glory as the sun rose through the trees.

The view will be different. The sun will rise either way. The choice is up to you.

As she heard God whisper the words, she finally understood that it really was her choice.

"But why are You giving me this choice? Why not just tell me what Your will for me is?" Callie spoke the question into the stillness.

Because this is about burial. Not of you, but of the grief you have still held onto. This is about burial of the past. I love you, and you should be able to choose where you want to do this. In full view of others or under cover, privately. The sun will still rise either way.

Everything came into focus. Callie realized what she wanted to do.

ಐಲ

On September 17th, Callie sat beside Monica in the truck once again, driving up the mountain to the small prayer cabin Papa had reminded her of. She clutched the tear-stained letter Papa had told her to write to the baby she had lost.

They were going to the prayer cabin's Grieving Pool.

The radio began playing "Friend of a Wounded Heart." Callie laughed. "Where did that come from? That's the song that kept playing when I was first going to counseling."

My love is going to spread across this land like a wildfire. Papa's voice echoed in her ears, but her stomach quivered, as tears began to form in her eyes. Dust clouds followed the truck down the long drive to the property.

"I like this land." Monica said cheerfully. "There are angels all over this place. I can feel them."

As they took the solemn stroll down a dirt path through the woods to the Grieving Pool, Callie's mind flashed back again.

Darkness closed in around her. The branches of fir trees caught her white robe as others with torches yelled and pulled her closer to the river's edge. Her little sister held tightly against her will, struggled behind her, fighting the arms of her assailant. Muffled screams turned to eerie silence. She carried the bundle wrapped tightly in her own arms. The gurgling water of the mighty Ohio River was the only other sound now.

Suddenly she came to. She shook herself. Blankly she announced to Monica, "I have to bury the letter alone."

A nod from her friend said enough.

Callie dug a hole at the roots of an old oak tree, silently mingling her tears with the dirt. Then she opened the letter, read aloud the words she'd written to the child she had lost, and carefully buried it, never to be seen again.

While Monica knelt by the Grieving Pool, patiently waiting, Callie sat down on an old bench. She pulled out three of the red roses she had brought and clutched them in her hand.

She had seen herself releasing the rose petals into the Grieving Pool. But now her heart was filled with doubt. *What difference will this make?*

Let them go, Callie.

Finally she stepped into the water.

"Look up, Callie," Monica called. "There's a ring of light above your head. Can you see it? It's amazing."

As Callie squinted up into the brilliance, the rose petals slipped slowly from her fingers, gently floating on top of the water.

"Father," she prayed, "to the best of my ability I release to You all the grief of the past. I release this child to You and every child who has been offered as a sacrifice. Please cut me and my family free from any ties to these sins or the consequences of them. I know You have already forgiven me, and I fully receive that."

As Callie's words lifted to heaven, she felt a great weight roll off her shoulders. The dragon lay dead at her feet.

It's done. It's done.

Monica still quietly crouched next to her.

"Callie, as you were releasing those things, I saw us standing here and on the Indian burial mounds next to the Ohio River, both places at once. I saw shadowy figures floating up, and Jesus was kneeling in front of you, facing you the whole time."

Tears of joy trickled down Callie's cheeks. Monica's eyes glistened as well.

"Time to go higher and celebrate," Monica proclaimed. They hopped back in the truck and drove up winding roads to the summit of the mountain.

As they stood on the pinnacle, overlooking their home, Callie heard words ringing in her ears.

This is my land. This is your land. The land receives you now.

"I finally belong somewhere," said Callie. "I finally have a family. I finally belong."

Monica grabbed her hand and held it up high. "You did it my friend. You did it. I'm so proud of you."

As the setting sun blazed behind them, they turned to go, but the strumming of a guitar stopped them in their tracks. On the rock below, a bearded man with his young daughter leaning against him strummed on his guitar and singing.

Callie gasped. "He's singing 'You Are My Sunshine.' It's what my grandpa used to sing to me when I was a little girl."

She breathed a deep sigh, as she realized it was a kiss from her true Father. "He does love me, doesn't He?"

"Yes, Callie. He does." Monica lovingly patted Callie on the shoulder.

As they drove back, Monica said, "Callie, you thought God was asking you to build an altar so you would fall on it, and if we had gone to the actual ground where the abuse happened that's what it would have felt like to you. But instead, when you built the altar here, God sent His fire on that altar. He already provided the sacrifice through His Son, Jesus."

That evening, Callie sat with Greg on the couch, retelling him all the wonderful things God had done. As she tilted her head up to gaze into his tender eyes, the girls peeked through the doorway, and Greg motioned for them to come. Running forward, they flung their open arms around their parents.

Callie looked up from the giant group hug. "Greg," she said over her daughters' giggles, "there's one more thing I need to do. I've got to go talk to Mom."

The next morning, she drove to her mother's retirement home and quietly opened the door of her apartment.

"Mom, are you up?" she called softly, hoping not to startle her. Her eyes adjusted to the dim light, and she made out the silhouette of her mother hunched over a box of photos.

"Oh Callie, come on in." Mama's voice broke as she sighed. "I miss your Me-Ma so much."

"Mom, do you look at the pictures all the time to try to remember the good times?"

"Yes, baby, it's all I have to hold onto."

Callie hesitated a few moments before continuing. "Mom, you know I remember now. I remember a lot. The good and the bad."

Mama clutched the pictures in her hands, keeping her gaze down, as Callie came up behind her and kissed the thin white hair on her head. "Mom, I do remember, but Jesus has healed my heart."

The words lingered in the air. She rubbed the center of her mom's back, feeling the bones through the worn nightgown. "Mom, I forgive you. I don't hold anything against you." As Callie's mom turned around in her chair, she saw the tears gathering in her mother's empty eyes.

Callie leaned down to embrace her. "I love you Mom. I always will."

God is a good, good Father, and His love will never leave me. He is making me whole.

No one could ever take that away from her now. No person or demon from hell could ever separate her from such an amazing love.

Epilogue

Dear Reader,

This story is based on a true account. The names, places, and time frames have been changed to protect Callie and those who know her.

Though the evils of secret societies are all around us, this story is not meant to stir fear, but to bring light into the darkness. It's time to step into the light, so healing can happen.

For those who have been silenced, who have been told lies similar to the ones Callie heard, this book is for you. Dear one, there is no wound so deep He can't heal. No mountain is too high that He wouldn't climb it to rescue you, no pit too deep He can't reach in and pull you out of. He loves you! Call out to Him. He will show you the way and timing of His unique rescue plan for you.

For the abuser, there is forgiveness if you are willing to turn from the hate. He sees the hurt, angry child inside, and He gave His life to rescue you. Surrender to Jesus.

For my Native American and African American brothers and sisters who have endured the hate of racism, Callie understands you better than most, because she felt your pain. It's time for forgiveness, reconciliation, and healing. You are deeply loved by your Father God, and in all your suffering He has been there. He will make it all right in the end. Trust Him.

There are many ways to healing. The path of inner healing Callie experienced is one way God led her into the truth of His love. It's not the way for everyone. The path of healing for satanic ritual abuse survivors and those suffering from dissociative disorders can be a long, hard road to wholeness, but it is worth it. In the next section I have included several different ministries with helpful resources for healing the broken ones, especially the least of these.

Whatever path God takes you on, He is the healer. He loves you, dear one.

Isaiah 51:1-4 tells why He came:

"[T] Lord has anointed Me to bring good news to the poor, He has sent Me to bind up the brokenhearted, to proclaim liberty to the captives, and the opening of the prison doors to those who are bound, to proclaim the year of the Lord's favor, and the day of vengeance of our God; to comfort all those who mourn . . . to give them a beautiful headdress instead of ashes, the oil of gladness instead of mourning, the garment of praise instead of a spirit of heaviness; that they may be called oaks of righteousness, the planting of the Lord, that He may be glorified. They shall rebuild the ancient ruins; they shall raise up the former devastation of many generations."

May Jesus heal our hearts, returning the voices of those who have been silenced.

As He crushes the great serpent-dragon under our feet.

Much love,
Charisse

Resources

Every journey towards freedom in Jesus is unique. These are books, websites, organizations, and ministries that may be of help. We don't necessarily agree with all the content, but our hope is that there will be aspects from some that will minister to you and others. We are praying for your guidance as you follow Jesus towards healing for yourself and/or others.

Books

Freedom: Coming out from under the Curses of Freemasonry by Samantha Mahoney

Uncovering the Mystery of MPD by James Friesen

The Truth about False Memory Syndrome by James Friesen

Soul Ties: The Unseen Ties in Relationship by David Cross

The Bondage Breaker by Neil Anderson

Victory Over the Darkness by Neil Anderson

Tear Down This Wall of Silence: Dealing with Sexual Abuse in Our Churches by Dale Ingraham and Rebecca Davis

How to Hear God's Voice by Mark and Patti Virkler

Mending the Soul by Steven R. Tracy and Celestia G. Tracy

The Broken Way by Ann Voscamp

Untwisting Scriptures that were used to tie you up, gag you, and tangle your mind by Rebecca Davis

Stand and Deliver by Tim and Beth Scott

Healing Through Deliverance by Peter Horrobin

Deliverance and Inner Healing by John and Mark Sandford

Hinds' Feet on High Places by Hannah Hurnard

Redeeming Love by Francine Rivers
The Final Quest by Rick Joyner
Uncle Tom's Cabin by Harriet Beecher Stowe
Blessing Your Body by Dr. Pamela LeGate
Blessing Your Spirit by Arthur Burke and Sylvia Gunter
Strategies for DID by Arthur Burke (CD series)
Restoring Survivors of Satanic Ritual Abuse by Patricia Clark
Multiple Identities: Understanding and Supporting the Severely Abused by Diane Hawkins
The Subtle Power of Spiritual Abuse by Johnson and van Vonderen
Boundaries by Cloud and Townsend
Dissociative Identity Disorder and Severe Childhood Abuse by Friesen and Flanagan (CD series)

Organizations Specializing in Helping Human Trafficking Survivors

Switch www.switchsc.org
National Center on Sexual Explotation
  www.endsexualexploitation.org
The Polaris Project www.polarisproject.org
The End It Movement www.enditmovement.com
Shared Hope www.sharedhope.org

Organizations and Ministries for Abuse Survivors

Word of God Prayer Ministry www.wogcounseling.org
Restoration in Christ Ministries www.rcm-usa.org
Heart Sync Ministry www.heartsyncministries.org

Immanuel Approach Ministry www.immanuelapproach.com

International Society of Deliverance Ministers
www.isdministers.org

DR Hodges, PO Box 222, Valentine, SC 296002, email
Is61WholeHeartHealing@outlook.com

Rape, Abuse, and Incest National Network www.rainn.org

The National Suicide Prevention Hotline 1-800-273-8255
The crisis text lines: text HOME to 741741

GRACE www.netgrace.org

SNAP Network www.snapnetwork.org

Darkness to Light Ministry www.d2l.org

The Hope of Survivors www.thehopeofsurvivors.org

Speaking Truth in Love Ministries www.speakingtruthinlove.org

Mending the Soul www.mendingthesoul.org

Life Model www.lifemodel.org

Dr. Diane Langberg www.dianelangberg.com

His Presence Online www.hispresenceonline.org

Help for Native American and African American Abuse Survivors

Strong Hearts Helpline www.strongheartshelpline.org

School of Wisdom and Higher Learning Bible Institute email
schoolofwisdomlearning714@gmail.com

Help for Spouses of Abuse Survivors

Marriage Reconstruction Ministries
www.marriagereconstructionministries.org

Help for Repentant Offenders

Broken Yoke Ministries www.brokenyoke.org

Other Helpful Resources

Here's the Joy www.heresthejoy.com
The Other Side of Darkness www.theothersideofdarkness.com
Elijah House Ministries www.elijahhouse.org
Sapphire Leadership Group www.theslg.com
Ellel Ministries www.ellel.org
Transformation Prayer Ministry www.transformationprayer.org
Bride Ministries International www.bridemovement.com
Deeper Walk International www.deeperwalkinternational.org

For other resources and more information about the author, please visit www.forthesilencedones.com and our Facebook page For the Silenced Ones.

Made in the USA
Las Vegas, NV
23 January 2022